Praise for Take Off!

"Marissa wants to fly but she's g[...] [...] [...] before she can take wing. That r[...] [...] camp, which takes on a whole new high-stakes meaning in Lea Beddia's exhilarating new novel." ~Tim Wynne-Jones, author of THE STARLIGHT CLAIM

"Take Off! is a fast-paced adventure story that will engage young readers, especially those with an interest in wilderness survival or aviation. Beddia cleverly uses flying as a metaphor for the ups and downs of complicated relationships, like the one between bully and target. A page-turner that will engage and enlighten young readers." ~Lori Weber, author of THE RIBBON LEAF (nominated for the 2023 Red Maple Award) <www.lori-weber.com>

"In this wonderful novel, Lea Beddia kicks-the-tires-and-lights-the-fires. In addition to enjoying the suspense and humour in Take Off! readers are sure to fall in love with this novel's fascinating, diverse cast of characters. I'm already looking forward to Beddia's next book!" ~Monique Polak, author of 32 books for young readers, including her most recent, THE BRASS CHARM

"I devoured this page-turner in one-sitting and was brought to my feet in a standing ovation. I love the protagonist – self-doubting and vulnerable, yet resilient with an inner courage impossible not to admire. There are coping strategies, here, to help deal with real-life bullies and steer the course through a complex of contemporary problems. Y.A. fiction? This is a Guide-to-Surviving-and-Thriving-Adolescence, and this adult could take a few pages out of this book. You landed it, Lea Beddia. Keep 'em coming." ~Darlene Madott, award-winning author of 9 books including, WINNERS AND LOSERS

Take Off!

BY
LEA BEDDIA

Published by Rebel Mountain Press, 2023
Copyright © 2023 by Lea Beddia

Cover Design & Layout-Cheryl Ann Kelly, Rebel Mountain Press
Edited by Lori Shwydky, Rebel Mountain Press

Library and Archives Canada Cataloguing in Publication

Title: Take off! / Lea Beddia.
Names: Beddia, Lea, author.
Identifiers: Canadiana 20220423512 | ISBN 9781989996133 (softcover)
Classification: LCC PS8603.E42435 T35 2023 | DDC jC813/.6—dc23

Printed and bound in Canada

ISBN 978-1-989996-13-3 (softcover)
Rebel Mountain Press—Nanoose Bay, BC, Canada

*We gratefully acknowledge that we are located on the traditional territory of the Snaw-
Naw-As First Nation.*

We gratefully acknowledge the support of

Supported by the Province of British Columbia

www.rebelmountainpress.com

Dedicated to you, dear reader.

May your dreams always soar beyond

the sky's limit.

CHAPTER ONE

D is for Dummy

High school is survival of the meanest. So far, I'm getting crushed by Aimee Ladouceur.

When we were still friends, we used to laugh about her name. It was perfect because in French, *Aimee* means loved and *Ladouceur* means gentleness. But not anymore. Nothing could be further from the truth these days.

"*D*? You got a *D*?" Aimee hovers over my shoulder and laughs so hard she snorts. "I wonder what that could stand for. *D* as in Dummy or *D* as in Dyke?"

I turn over my essay so she can't read Ms. Hillebrand's comments. I want to roll it up and smack her with it, but I hold back and watch Aimee strut to her friend's desk, showing off her essay. Her long, dark hair is down around her shoulders in loose curls. When she picks up her school bag, her arm muscles flex. She's strong, and tall, with legs longer than sunflower stems.

"I thought you pulled an all-nighter to finish this last week," Rock says, tapping me on the shoulder.

It's the end of class and Ms. Hillebrand is letting us chat. "I did. That's the problem. I suck under pressure." I fold the essay and stuff it into my bag. "My mom's going to flip."

"At least it's a pass," Rock reassures me. "Once you pass your test flight tomorrow, she'll be too proud to care about an essay."

"I'm not so sure," I say. "I'm flunking. How am I supposed to fly tomorrow when I can't even write a stupid essay?"

"They're two different things. Besides, we went over the flight guide a gazillion times. You wrote your essay in a hurry. The test flight will be fine. You know your stuff."

That's easy for Rock to say. Studying and school come easy for him. I have to work twice as hard to catch up to him. But at least he's a great study partner.

"What time should we pick up you and your mom tomorrow?" he asks.

"Early. Like, seven." I want to get to the airfield early to watch planes take off and land, while I run procedures in my head. "My test is at nine. You?"

"Just before yours. I'll be able to watch you land."

Rock and I have been in cadets together since we were thirteen. From the first time we rode together as passengers in a glider, we both knew we wanted to fly, and we have spent every free moment since then learning and training for tomorrow's test. If we pass, we'll each have our private license.

Mom is a little freaked out I'll be able to fly a plane before I'm allowed to drive a car, but it is the thing I want most in the world.

"All right, now what do I do about this? I say, showing him my essay. "A '*D*' means I might not even pass this course. I'm failing history, too. What if I don't graduate?"

"You're getting a little panicky. There's extra credit stuff you can do."

"More essays? That might be your thing."

"There's the end of year trip. The survival camp thing," Rock says.

"Isn't that just for phys. ed?"

"We could transfer credits."

"How do you know all this?" I ask, suspicious.

"I had a feeling you might need the extra help. Don't get mad. I went to see the guidance counsellor to ask. Just in case."

"Wow. Thanks for your undying love and confidence," I say.

"Hey. I'm a realist."

"Fine, sign me up," I say, faking enthusiasm.

"Don't be so bitter. A weekend of camping and hiking. With me. It'll be the easiest make-up test ever."

Rock is right. If all I have to do is pitch a tent, hike a trail, and play survival games to gain my credits, it isn't anything I haven't already done with cadets.

"You'll come too, right?" I ask.

"Of course," he says. "Wouldn't leave you alone in the woods for a second with your terrible sense of direction."

"You're hilarious." I give him a playful punch on the shoulder.

The bell rings and we file out of class to leave. Aimee stands behind me, waiting to get past. "Out of my way, L'Heureux," she says to me. "Some of us have a life to get to."

I have no comeback, and she's too quick, anyway; she disappears down the hall.

"Focus," Rock says, watching me as my blood boils. "By this time tomorrow, we'll both be licensed pilots."

I hope he's right.

CHAPTER TWO

Cross Winds

Rock gives me a thumb's up from the cockpit.

I was up late yesterday revising my flight manual and aviation guides. Rock and I video chatted and tested each other. I was too wired to sleep, but when Mom came to my room around midnight with melatonin and a glass of water, she insisted I get some rest.

Rock's takeoff is perfect. I lose sight of him as he flies off, and Commander Hensen approaches me.

"Ready, Marisa?" she says, her clipboard in hand. We cross over to the Cessna parked across from the hangar. She watches as I go through my checklist. Everything is ready. We sit in the cockpit and when Commander Hensen gives me the go-ahead, I start the engine. The vibrations are exhilarating and familiar.

The propeller spins as we double-check our seat belts. My arms prickle with nerves and excitement. If I pass this test, I'll be the first girl in this squadron to have a private license. No pressure, *just have fun*, I repeat to myself.

The plane is in full throttle. Oil pressure and temperature are normal. "Airspeed alive," I report to Commander Hensen. I'm ready for my test flight.

"You've got this, Marisa. Just have fun," Commander Hensen says. Her voice is confident, calm, and encouraging.

*

The takeoff is clean with just the right amount of wind. We fly over checkered farmlands. Long, rectangular plots of green and khaki spread out from the river; potato and cornfields first cultivated by French settlers. The map of this landscape dates back to New France. The view is my favourite part: a map in three dimensions. I can get lost in it and forget time—that is, until the wind hits the wings, and we teeter.

"Nice and smooth, like you've practiced," Commander Hensen says. I move the ailerons to level the wings and stabilize with the yoke. My whole body is energized. *I'm doing it!* A few miles out, the mountains appear in the distance.

Commander Hensen gives me coordinates to follow our flight path. The land changes from the fertile fields of the St. Lawrence lowlands to the green blanketed hills of the Canadian Shield. Eskers—rock and sediment left over from the last ice age—form ridges like interlocking fingers. They fold into each other with streams flowing in between.

It's so beautiful, I could stay up here forever. At 2000 feet, Commander Hensen says, "Monitor your fuel." I checked it before takeoff, but it's decreased since then. I should have noticed without her reminding me. I'll lose points for this.

Commander Hensen strains her neck back and up. "There's fuel spilling," she says. "What do you need to remember?" Her voice is much calmer than my heartbeat.

"Aviate, navigate, communicate," I say, recalling my training.

"What's first?"

"I have to . . . get fuel." I'm drawing a blank. I feel so stupid. I should react quickly.

"Right, so what steps do you take to aviate?"

I'm in a freeze-frame, staring at the fuel gauge, which is telling me we're leaking.

"Switch fuel tank," I yell.

"Good."

I can't believe I hesitated, but I'm back on track and I draw fuel from the right tank, keeping control of the plane. I know it's important to stay calm, but I'm having trouble. I'm sweating and my hands are shaky.

"That's it. Let's keep going," Commander Hensen says, and we carry on with our flight. When she instructs us to prepare for landing, I look at our GPS and map to make sure we are on the right path toward the runway. The skies are clear, and there are no clouds. One little hiccup, but now I'm confident today will end with me as a licensed pilot.

"What if you had to have an emergency landing? Can you simulate your distress call for me?"

I recall the phonetic alphabet I learned in cadets to communicate the plane's registration code.

"I would signal: 'Mayday, Mayday, Mayday.
This is Cessna one-seven-two. G-I-L-C
GOLF INDIA LIMA CHARLIE
GOLF INDIA LIMA CHARLIE
GOLF INDIA LIMA CHARLIE
2000 feet, one mile north of Joliette.
Fuel leak.
Will perform an emergency landing.
Two souls on board.
White and red aircraft.'"

I know I nailed it.

"Exactly. Let's see you land on the runway," Commander Hensen says.

I'm beaming, and by now, I'm certain the fuel leak was a planned part of the test. Despite my hesitation and nerves, I followed all the right steps. We fly straight toward the runway and descend. I lower the flaps to slow down the plane. I'm almost done, but before I can sigh with relief, a rough crosswind catches us. The nose wheel touches down on the runway too early. The pitch-down is too strong. The plane jerks and shoves us around the small cockpit. I brace myself with my hands tight around the yoke.

We stop moving suddenly. Blood rushes to my head, making me feel heavy. My eyes feel like they might pop out of their sockets. I try to orient myself and realize we've flipped. We're upside down in our plane! I need to get out. This isn't safe. I need to leave. Now.

I'm so tightly secured in my seat I can barely move. My seat belt digs into my ribs. I expect to have Commander Hensen tell me what to do next, but she's unconscious, her hair suspended in front of her eyes. Her head is bleeding.

We need to get out!

I grope and fumble for the latch to release my seatbelt, but it won't come off. I open the Swiss Army knife in my pocket and saw through the strap. I land hands and knees onto the windshield. This is a small airport, with no traffic controller on sight. The cadets and commanders are at the other end of the airfield. They may have seen the landing but are too far away to help. I'm about to unhitch Commander Hensen's belt, but she'll hit her head. And I can't carry her out alone, so I take hold of the radio instead, hoping to signal to a nearby pilot.

"Mayday, Mayday, Mayday."

CHAPTER THREE

Picking up the Pieces

A siren blares. Voices yelling. The plane door opens. Someone grabs me from under my arms. Two other people unlatch Commander Hensen. She comes to, slowly. She's confused. A concussion, someone says. I'm sat down on a stretcher. I lie down. The sky is blue. I close my eyes. A paramedic asks me questions. What day it is, my name, all things I know.

"Commander Hensen?" I ask.

"She'll be okay," the paramedic says. "But they're taking her to the hospital. For observation. Don't worry." He shines a light in my eyes and tells me to follow his finger.

"It was my fault," I say.

"I doubt it," the paramedic says. "You can come over," he says over my shoulder, "She's fine." I sit up and Rock and Mom are running toward me. Mom's got me in a death squeeze and I can hardly breathe.

"I'm fine," I say to her, but she doesn't let go right away.

Rock waits patiently. His embrace is much gentler. He rubs my back, pulls away slightly and looks at me.

"It'll be fine," he says, knowing my worry. "Commander will be fine."

"Can we take her home?" Mom asks the paramedic.

"She's good to go," he says. "Just keep an eye on her for signs of concussion, but I think she's in the clear."

"Good. We can go home," Mom says.

"Wait," Rock says. "We have to wait."

"For what?" Mom pulls at the strap of her purse. "She needs to rest."

"They want to question Commander Hensen. Find out what happened. They told us to sit tight, until then."

"That's ridiculous."

"Mom, it's fine. I'm fine." She looks at me skeptically. Even I don't believe myself.

"Hungry?" she asks me.

I shrug. There's no way I can eat, but I could use a little less Mom right now.

"I can do a Tim's run. Coffee or hot chocolate?"

"Hot chocolate," I say. Rock holds up two fingers.

"You sure you're fine?" she asks again.

"We have to wait. So, we'll wait. We might as well have snacks," Rock says.

"Okay. I'll be back in about fifteen minutes," Mom says, and I'm surprised we've actually convinced her to leave.

I sit on the couch in the hangar closest to where I crash-landed. Normally, other cadets would be milling around, excited about their test flights, waiting nervously, but the place has been cleared. There is me, Rock, and a maintenance crew. Crew members run in and out. I dare to look at the runway. Our plane is still there. The right wing in pieces on the tarmac. My stomach churns and lurches, like I'm still in movement.

"You going to be sick or something?" Rock says.

"I'm okay. I just can't believe it. I messed up big time."

"No way. We saw the landing. Strong crosswinds. Only so much you can do, Marisa."

"I wasn't in control."

Rock doesn't say anything, and I'm grateful. I notice the lapel of his uniform. A pin with silver wings has been added to his uniform. "Hey. You did it!" I say, finally realizing he passed his test flight before my disaster. "Congrats."

"Thanks."

"There is no way they'll give me my wings after today."

"Let's just wait and see," Rock says. "You can take the test again."

"There's no way Mom can afford it. I'm done," I say.

We sit in silence. We watch the crew pick up the pieces of the plane on the tarmac. I feel like everything inside of me that worked and studied and trained is in pieces, too. I can't believe I failed.

Footsteps echo in the hangar. When I look up, Commander Arnold is marching toward us. Rock and I stand and salute him.

"How is Commander Hensen?" Rock asks.

"She's fine. Slight concussion, but she'll fully recover." He looks to me. "She told us the crosswinds were strong during landing. You did all you could do, Marisa. Your test won't count. I'll be in touch about when we can reschedule your test." We salute him and he marches off.

"See, it'll be fine."

"It's not fine. Crosswinds or no crosswinds, I lost control of the plane. I messed up. I failed."

"So we study harder and get you ready for your next test. You have a second chance."

"I can't. I mean, look at what I did." I point to the debris on the runway. "I can't go through with that again."

"Maybe you just need some time. We'll figure it out. Promise." Rock wraps his arm around me, and lets me curl into him. He lets me cry without trying to stop me. He hands me my hot chocolate when Mom arrives and whispers something to her to let her know not to say a word on the long drive home.

CHAPTER FOUR

Ice Cream Fixes Everything

"It's been a week," Mom says, from the other side of my closed door. A week of feeling like a total disaster and failure. "You need to get out."

"And go where?" I yell through the door.

"Anywhere. Outside. To a party. Just . . . go."

I open the door and she almost stumbles in. "Why are you so keen on getting rid of me?" I ask.

"That's not it," she says, leading me to the kitchen. She pours herself a cup of coffee. "But it's Saturday. Shouldn't you be at the mall, or with Rock, or . . ." she slurps her coffee. "Or with some girls?" she says, raised eyebrows visible over her cup.

I try really hard to let my eyes roll all the way to the back of my head. "Please, don't," I say.

"There's no one you have your eye on?"

"Okay. I'll go out. So long as we don't have to talk. I'll get dressed."

"Is talking to me so bad?"

"Talking to you about girls is bad."

Mom sits, opening her *L'actualité* news magazine. "We can talk politics," she says, holding up the magazine.

"Better, but I'm still going out." I head to my room, and text Rock to meet me at the park. We can take public transport into town and go to the mall. There isn't anything else to do in our town hidden in the folds of cornfields and valleys. The mall is as good as it gets. It's a forty-minute bus ride to Joliette. Rock and I listen to our favourite classic rock playlist. We barely ever talk on the bus. We listen and people-watch, which is the way I like it.

When we step off the bus to walk to the mall, Rock finally asks, "Why the sudden urge to shop today?"

"My mom wanted me out of the house."

"She told you to leave?"

"Sort of. She started asking me about girls."

Rock gasps, faking shock. "How terrible; a mother interested in her daughter's love life."

"Or lack thereof. Besides, I don't have anything to say, and she's always trying to talk about how I feel." We cross through the parking lot toward the entrance.

"So tell her the truth."

"There is nothing to tell. I messed up on my test flight. End of story."

"And we came to the mall, which we hate. Did you want to come to watch all the pretty girls walk by?"

"Shut up," I say, pushing him playfully. I open the door to the building. I hold it open for a mother carrying several bags and a screaming toddler.

"So why are we here?" he asks.

"I need new hiking boots," I say, which is true, except that gets me thinking about cadets, and that gets me depressed again.

"How about ice cream first?" Rock suggests. "On me."

We sit in the food court, eating our gelato when he finally brings it up, but unlike Mom, Rock has a way of making everything feel natural. "It'll be fine, you know. You'll take the test again. You'll pass with flying colours."

"I don't know if I can."

"I've seen you fly. And we'll study some more to make sure you're prepared."

"I don't know if I can get in a plane again." I bite into my cone and keep the gelato from escaping over the sides.

"Crosswinds, Marisa. They happen. It wasn't your fault."

"I know, but that crosswind happened to destroy the plane I was in."

"We should go flying."

"What?"

"The longer you're away from it, the harder it'll be. It's like when my dad got into his accident. He insisted on getting behind the wheel the next day. He said if he didn't, he may never want to again."

"He's a truck driver, that's different. He had to."

"And you're a pilot," Rock says.

"Not yet," I remind him.

"You're a pilot. You know it."

"In any case, Mom won't let me fly again unless I pull up my grades. I get another shot at the test, but I still have to pay for it. Mom has to pay for it, and she's not going to dish out the extra cash if I don't graduate first."

"There's a month left of school. We'll study like crazy for exams."

"Easy for you," I say. "I'm way behind in a bunch of classes. If I flunk one exam, I'm done for."

"So we'll do the survival camp. Easy credits."

"You don't need them," I say. I point to where he's got chocolate mint chip dripping from his chin.

"It'll be fun," Rock says. "Maybe a good way to get you back into the right mindset for another test flight." He pulls a napkin from the dispenser and wipes his face clean.

"You're right," I say.

"Of course I'm right. And it'll keep you out of your Mom's line of firing questions, and get you out of the house like she wants. Win-win."

"And I'll get to wear my new boots," I say, taking the last bite of my cone.

"See? Ice cream fixes everything," Rock says.

CHAPTER FIVE

Tripping Up

At school, Rock and I sign up for survival camp. Mr. Belisle, the phys. ed teacher, hands us permission forms to sign. Mom is excited, and signs it the second I show her. Rock suggested a week ago that I start packing, but as usual, I've left if for the last second.

"Don't forget your new hiking boots," he tells me Friday after school. We stand at our lockers and, for once, I know I won't have to worry about homework. I make sure I have my book to read on the bus. I don't read much and it takes me forever to finish something, but Mom got me Chris Hadfield's *An Astronaut's Guide to Life on Earth,* and I love it. He describes his experiences as a fighter pilot and I can't put it down.

As I pack up, Aimee pushes past me, and I stumble, face first into my locker. Her dark curls swoosh behind her, like a basketball through a net.

"She did that on purpose," Rock says.

It's hard to tell. Aimee whipped her bag over her shoulder and caught me off guard.

"Push back, Marisa. You can take her," Rock continues, turning me in her direction. Lockers clang shut around us as students head out to catch their buses.

Rock is right; I could take her. I won all the physical training tests in our cadets' survival activities. I even outlasted some of the boys, but Aimee is more than muscle and strength. She digs into something inside me, under my skin where no one else can reach.

Our friendship ended in third grade, but I've never been able to put my finger on what happened. Lately, it seems I've been on the receiving end of a lot of accidental pushes and shoves from her. Only Rock knows how Aimee treats me. He's like my brother and I trust him not to blab, but he doesn't understand why Aimee can wreck me with one smug glance. Neither do I.

"Hitting her back would make it worse, and you know it," I tell Rock. "Besides, I don't fight."

"Then tell someone, already." He looks at himself in his mirror and dabs some concealer under his eyes, as if he needs it. His eyes are so dark and pretty with long feathery lashes, no one would notice the bags under them. Satisfied, he turns to me. "Look up," he says, holding my forehead up against his palm, so he can apply some eyeliner. He thinks it makes my eyes pop, but I hate the feeling of gunk on my eyes. My eyes do look amazing with it, though, with the green really coming through. He tugs at my braid, but it's too hot to let my frizzy hair go wild and free. I slap his hand away.

"Those golden locks, gone to waste," he says.

"Who can I tell about Aimee? Mr. George, the guidance counsellor slash tech teacher? I already tried." A few months ago, Aimee slammed her cafeteria tray into me *by mistake*, splattering ketchup and shepherd's pie all over my new hoodie. I complained to Mr. George about it. He said to give her the benefit of the doubt. But she kept coming after me. Once, Mr. George passed us as Aimee opened her locker in my face, a wily smile across her lips. He hurried down the hall, pretending not to notice. Then Aimee and her sorority of basketball players followed me into the bathroom where she knocked me into the tampon dispenser. Again, making it seem like an accident. The dispenser cracked open, tampons rolling to the ground.

"You can tell your parents," Rock says.

"They're still dealing with the lesbian thing. My mom will blow a fuse."

"They seemed pretty cool with it." Rock offers me a ruby-red lip gloss. I shake my head no, so he tries a clear gloss, and I accept. He rolls his eyes at me, but applies it for me anyway.

"Yeah, but they've been checking up on all my social media and asking about school. It's annoying. If I tell them about this, they'll never let me out of their sight. Besides, there's only one more month of school left. I can deal," I say.

"I might take Aimee on myself if she does this again," Rock says, flexing his biceps. Rock is taller than I am, by a foot, with an athletic build most girls swoon over. I squeeze his bicep, pretend it's hot, and shake my hand out. He smiles and blows on his muscles, like he's cooling them down, then sweeps his brown hair out of his eyes. He's due for a haircut. "At least we'll have some time away from her at survival camp. It's gonna be so perfect!" But before Rock is done packing up his makeup, Aimee returns, opens her locker, pulls something out and into her backpack, then slams it shut again.

"Nice purse," Aimee says walking up to Rock. She's almost as tall as he is. She pulls Rock's makeup case to the floor. Rock bends down to pick up his eyeliner and shadows.

She crosses her arms and kicks a rolling lip gloss farther away from him. Her oversized bag is bright red and bulging.

"You stuff an eighth-grader in there? Saving it for your supper?" Rock says before we head outside, Aimee ahead of us.

She stops, then pivots to smile at Rock. It's a bright smile, but her eyes are deadpan and the contrast gives me shivers. "Camping gear," she says, orbiting around us, dribbling her basketball. "For this weekend. Survival camp." She fakes a shot at Rock's face and we both flinch.

I groan. I don't mean to, but it escapes me. Her grin widens. She tilts her head and speaks an octave higher, like she's talking to a baby. "Scared?" she asks, holding her ball still while she waits for me to answer.

It never occurred to me she'd be on this trip. Her satisfied smirk gives me goosebumps and I could scream for allowing myself to be blindsided like this.

"Nah," I try to sound cool. "Survival is in my blood."

"We'll see," she says, scanning me up and down like she's ready to make me bleed to prove it. She lines up for the bus as it screeches to a stop.

I thought camp would be easy credits. I mean, I've done cadets since I was thirteen, not to mention my survival and pilot training. But navigating a plane is nothing compared to navigating Aimee Ladouceur.

Rock waves his hands, shepherding me onto our bus. "Why would she even want to come?" Rock whispers as we sit in our usual spots at the back.

"I guess she needs extra credits, too," I say, regretting my lack of motivation throughout the year. "Any other way for us to graduate?" I ask, desperate.

We both applied for the commercial piloting program at the college in Chicoutimi, and getting my license and logging hours would give me a head above the competition. I've worked so hard, late nights studying our aviation manual with

Rock, but I won't be accepted without my high school diploma. But when I imagine myself in a plane again, my skin gets hot and prickly.

"I'm not sure I'll make it," I say.

"What do you mean? Survival camp?"

"Test flight, college, graduation. All of it."

"You can do this!" Rock's voice is like a personal trainer, trying to motivate an out-of-shape trainee. When he sees I'm not in the mood for jokes, he lowers his voice. "Dealing with Aimee for a few days beats summer school," Rock says, and he's right. "Why does she have all her gear with her now, anyway?" he asks, watching Aimee spin a basketball on her index finger. I can't think of a reason why she'd drag all her equipment to school, then home again when we don't leave until tomorrow morning. "At least we'll be together. And she'll probably be too busy flirting with every boy there."

"Except you," I say, and Rock gives me an affectionate shove. Aimee dribbles her basketball in the aisle near the front of the bus. The muscles in her legs flex as she moves. She's fast and strong, but graceful, too. She'd probably outrun me in any race. Her short-shorts rise a little as she moves. I tug at my baggy cargo pants. She dribbles back and forth between the benches until the bus driver yells at her to cut it out.

"You're not going to back out, are you?" Rock says, snapping his fingers in my face.

I'm tempted to fake a flesh-eating disease, or catch a real one, if it means I won't have to spend the weekend in the woods with Aimee, but I need my credits. And Rock signed up, too, for me. With him there, it'll be okay.

When we reach our stop, I walk down the steps, but Rock trips and falls flat in the aisle. Aimee's sitting in her seat, her leg outstretched, pantomiming innocence with a shrug.

"You okay?" the bus driver asks. Rock waves him off and I can tell he's embarrassed and trying to hide it, the way he won't make eye contact. He stands and hops down the steps, one leg suspended in front of him. I reach out to help him down. The driver closes the door, but when Rock tries to put pressure on his hurt foot, there is a crack. He falls, hands spread out in front of him. The bus hurls off in a puff of black smoke, and I swear Aimee has her nose plastered to the window of the bus, watching. Laughing.

Living in the country is a drag most days, but especially when your bus driver abandons you between two cornfields.

Rock still hasn't stood up. "Are you okay?" I ask, but he's grabbing his foot and sucking air through his teeth.

"Do something," Rock pleads. I dial his mom's number and she arrives in a panic. I know how to wrap a sprained foot and I use his mom's silk scarf to help hold it in place. Once Rock has caught his breath, his mom and I help him into the passenger seat.

"Sorry Marisa, I'd give you a lift, but I think we need to go to the emergency room," Rock's mom says.

"I'll walk. Unless you want me to come?"

"I'll be fine," Rock says, but he's bent over in the seat still holding his ankle. "I'll call you later."

I close his door and wave. I'm left on a dirt road, dust rising as they drive away, with a mountain of worry building inside of me. How am I supposed to even think about heading to survival camp without my best defense?

CHAPTER SIX

Flying Solo

The next morning, Rock finally answers his phone after my twentieth attempt to video chat. His sleepy eyes pop up on my screen.

"I spent all night at the emergency room, and *you're* the one who's impatient?" he says, in a hoarse voice. He obviously didn't get much sleep.

"You didn't answer any of my texts," I say.

"My phone died. I'm fine, by the way. Thanks for asking."

"Right. Sorry. You need a cast or something?"

"Just a sprain, but I have to walk with crutches for a little while."

"Rockyyyy . . ." I whine.

"I know. I'm sorry. I can't do survival camp. Not unless you want to carry me on your back through the mountains. Sorry."

"This sucks."

"Are you even packed yet?" he asks.

"Almost." It's more of a question.

"Show me."

Clothes clutter my room. Rock helps me choose what to pack. I fill my bag with the essentials: socks, underwear, and a raincoat sealed in a compact case, no bigger than my palm to save space. I stop.

"I can't do this alone," I say. "Forget it." I turn my bag upside down and let everything fall onto my bed.

"Hold up," Rock says. "No way. You need this. It's bad enough that I can't go. If you were the one stuck at home, you'd have to write a ton of essays to make up your credits. Count yourself lucky."

"It's going to be horrible," I tell Rock.

"You're the bravest person I know. I'm not the only one who thinks it. You'll be fine."

"What's that supposed to mean?"

"Just that some of our fellow cadets think you should receive the Service Medal for Bravery."

"Are you insane? You saw what I did the last time I was in a plane!"

"I'm talking about what you did after your landing. Looking after Commander Hensen. Getting help. Anyone else would have frozen up."

"You call that a landing?"

"You have to move past it. It wasn't your fault. And I know you can handle Aimee."

He's doing his best to lighten me up, but I'm not courageous. I'm a wimp. When he mentions landing a plane, I shiver at the memory of metal scraping along the tarmac.

Hiding under the covers seems like a better option than being on my own at survival camp.

"Don't be late," he grumbles, scrunching his face like an old man and pointing a finger at my screen. He's so ridiculous.

"Anything else?" I say, packing up again.

"Yeah, one more thing." He pauses, waiting to make sure I'm listening. "Have fun."

"Right," I say and end our call. I search for extra socks in my drawer. I don't want wet feet if it rains this weekend. On my nightstand, in a frame my mother insists on displaying, is a picture of me and Rock in our cadet uniforms standing in front of a Cessna right before our first flights. My curly hair is pulled back in a bun. My uniform hat covers the frizz. Rock's dark hair is much shorter than it is now. He's let his bangs grow out since we took the picture. He'll probably cut it again in the summer to be clean cut again for cadets. We look happy. Hopeful. I turn the frame face down for the millionth time.

I should eat something to have enough energy for today, but if I do, I'm afraid it'll come flying right back up.

CHAPTER SEVEN

Amphibious Bully

Mom drops me off early at school to catch the bus to camp. She knows I'm upset about Rock not coming.

"Ready?" she asks, and I know she's hoping I'll open up to her.

"Sure," I lie. But I still can't force myself to open the door.

"What is it? You can tell me." Her hand is on my shoulder. I shrug it off. I hate when she tries to get all *let me in and tell me how you feel.* "You're worried about Rock?"

"Yeah," I answer, as Aimee and her friend Natasha approach the curb from down the street. They're shoving each other playfully as the bus rolls up.

"Is that Aimee?" Mom asks.

"She's in my class," I say.

"Wow. She's changed. She's so . . . tall. And . . . beautiful." She looks at me, and I stop watching Aimee. "You two still friends?"

"Nope."

"Do you . . . *like* her?"

"Oh my god, Mom, you're kidding me, right?"

"You're staring. I thought, maybe?"

"I don't like every girl, just because I'm gay."

"Okay, I'm sorry, but you had your awkward face."

Geez, Mom, I wonder why.

"I didn't mean to—" she stops herself mid-sentence. "I just meant, I know you're upset Rock won't be here, but you could use this weekend to make new friends," she says.

"Right," I mutter.

"And you need the credits."

"Yes, thanks for the reminder."

"I'm not trying to put you down."

But that's not how it feels. She's made it clear that if I don't graduate, there is no way she'll even consider dishing out the cash for me to take my test flight again. I'll have to get a summer job to help pay for it, and that can't happen if I'm in summer school. And if I want any chance of getting accepted to college, I'm going to have to suck it up and get through this weekend.

"You scared?"

"Why would I be?"

"This hiking and camping in the wilderness. You'll be pretty far away from everything."

"I've flown a plane. I can hike a trail."

"I know, I know. But it's okay to say you're scared." I stare her down. "All right, I'll let it go. Anything else?" she asks.

"Nope. I'm good. Bye Mom," I say, unbuckling my seat belt.

"Love you, kiddo," she says a little too loudly.

"Yeah, me too," I whisper.

I head to the bus, but then Mom calls out through her open window, loud enough for everyone to hear her, "Have fun!"

I hurry past Aimee and she mimics my mother, "Yeah, Marisa, have fun," she teases. She snorts and shoves me aside with the same overstuffed bag she carried yesterday.

I instinctively turn to make a snappy comment to Rock about her ultra-tight shorts and halter top, when I remember he's not here. I pretend to tie my shoelace, avoiding eye contact with her. The bus driver opens the doors to let us on and I can't help watching Aimee climb onto the bus.

"Quit staring, L'Heureux. For boys' eyes only," Aimee says, smacking her butt. And as I step onto the bus and dart past her, she holds my arm and whispers, so only I can hear, "No *dykes* allowed," and runs her hands along the curves of her body.

My cheeks burn. Hoping to disappear, I sit in an empty seat near the back. When I came out last year, some people called me brave, and some stopped talking to me. But Aimee uses every chance to remind everyone I'm gay and that she's out of my league. As if I'd be interested in a girl who makes my skin crawl. She reminds me of the snakes at the reptile zoo. They have beautiful colouring but nasty eyes and fangs, ready to strike.

"Where's Mr. Lipstick, or are you two no longer friends with benefits?" she calls out from the front.

Rock and I have kissed. Once. Like a year ago. We were outside the art studio after school when we thought everyone was gone. We agreed we should get some kissing experience and it would be less embarrassing to practice on each other for the first time than with anyone else. It was platonic and practical. We gave each other pointers on how to improve. Apparently, I was a little sloppy and should hold off on the Doritos before kissing anyone else. I told Rock his tongue was a little too swirly.

Aimee was leaving the gym after basketball practice and saw us. Of course, she twisted it into something else and now uses it against us any chance she finds. No witty insults come to mind, so I slump in my seat and pull out my book: Chris Hadfield's *An Astronaut's Guide to Life on Earth*. I intend to hide behind it for the next two hours.

"Can I sit here?" Dawn Morosa stands in the aisle, holding onto my bench as the bus lurches forward. Thick black makeup lines Dawn's eyes, giving her an alt-rock raccoon look. One side of her head is shaved close to the scalp and the other side coils in short curls, some purple popping out against her natural black, bouncing every time the bus drives over a pothole. Her Doc Marten combat boots are knee-high and bad-ass. She's wearing jeans cut off at her knees and a checkered shirt tied around her waist. A torn black T-shirt a size too big sits off her right shoulder.

"Sure," I say, which is probably more than I've said to her in the last five years. We used to play murder ball in grade school, but I doubt she remembers. We were supposed to kick the ball at someone as hard as we could and get them *out*. Dawn always just missed me. I was the only person she ever missed.

"What failure are you making up for?" Dawn asks.

"Failures. Plural," I scoff. "You?"

"Drama," Dawn says, eyeing Aimee. "Speaking of drama, I didn't think this would be *her* thing."

"You mean prancing around in short shorts, hooking up with every boy on the bus with limited adult supervision?" I ask.

Mr. Belisle, our chaperone for the weekend, is on his bench. All I can see from here is his bald spot and the huge earphones he's wearing, probably blasting heavy metal to drown us out, like he does while we're in P.E.

Dawn sits and opens a book with a bleeding skull on the cover, then doesn't say another thing to me for the next two hours. I don't think Dawn is looking for any friends on this trip, which makes me miss Rock even more.

We leave town on a road surrounded by nothing. After almost two hours, the bus bumps along gravel, lifting dust. We're on a constant incline up a winding road. My ears pop as we reach a higher altitude. There's nothing but forest outside as we get closer to our destination. It's far from home, remote, and perfect.

When we step off the bus, the soft ground is still muddy from the last time it rained. The air is perfumed with fresh pine, moss, and a slight, but not gross fishy smell from the river. It's humid, even though it's only ten o'clock in the morning and I'm grateful for the shady forest.

It's peacefully quiet. Until a too-cheery camp monitor, maybe a year or two older than us, greets our group.

"Good morning, hopeful survivors!" he says. He's wearing a *Camp du Nord* cap and T-shirt with a nametag dangling on a lanyard that reads *Jean-Paul*. "I'll escort you down the path to the campsite where you'll set up your tents. Chemical toilets are set up all over camp. Please use them. There is no running water on site, so be sure you have all your equipment, water and needs before we walk any farther." I tap the bottle in my side pocket. "After a tour of the grounds, we're going for a swim."

It's already hot and humid. A swim in the river would be a great way to get the bus smell out of my hair.

Jean-Paul continues, "After we cool off, I'll pair you up for your activities this weekend. Campfire tonight. Then a day-long hike tomorrow starting at . . ." he flips a page on his clipboard. "Six a.m." He looks at his phone. "The forecast is calling for rain in the afternoon, so be prepared."

Aimee grunts, then links arms with Natasha, who looks at the river with shifty eyes. Aimee pats her on the back.

Dawn stands closer to me. "Think we can pair up?" she asks. Dawn is probably the only person here who won't try to push my head underwater.

"Sure, if we can choose," I say.

We carry our equipment another half-hour uphill before reaching the campsite. Dawn is behind me, breathing heavily. Sweat forms behind my neck. Aimee walks past us, her friends struggling to keep up.

When we reach the campsite, I'm stunned by the beauty surrounding us. Water trickles down the rocks like a leaky faucet into a wide opening in the river. There's almost no current and it looks more like a lake. I studied Google Earth last night and know it's the widest point of the L'Assomption River. Mountains pointed with pine trees jet out across the river and reflect into the water. It's calm and so crisp I want to jump right in and disrupt the mirror surface. The sky is bright and blue, summer holidays just around the corner.

Jean-Paul shows us where we can set up our tents. Aimee approaches him with a whole bunch of questions, and he flips his clipboard then leads Aimee toward a clearing to her spot. His hand on the small of her back. Here three seconds and she's already flirting.

Overhead, a plane roars across the sky. Everyone cranes their neck up. It's white with a red cross on the side. It comes down low in a graceful sweep, grazing the water. It slows down and the floaters streak across the river, making waves as it lands upriver. It almost makes me miss being in a plane, but as the engine roars louder, I get anxious. My breath is caught in my lungs somewhere, and I sputter like an engine low on fuel. Dawn's hand is on my shoulder. I breathe, then cough to make it seem like I'm having a coughing fit instead of some kind of nervous breakdown.

"You all right?" Dawn asks.

"Yeah, fine," I say, holding my throat. "Swallowed a bug." I can tell Dawn doesn't buy it with her lopsided grin, but she doesn't push it, either.

"You afraid of planes, L'Heureux?" Aimee asks.

"What kind of plane is that?" Natasha asks, noticing the floaters.

"Hermaphrodite plane?" Aimee says.

"*Amphibious*," I correct her. "It can land on a runway and on water."

"Ooh, flies both ways, huh? You should know," Aimee says, looking at me as she walks past Dawn and me.

"What's that about?" Dawn asks.

"Nothing important."

"You think Aimee will be as horrible in the water as she is on land?"

"Yeah, an amphibious bitch," I say, and Dawn bubbles with laughs. It's enough to make me forget how badly I want to leave this place.

CHAPTER EIGHT

Standing Up

With humidity off the charts, the river is welcoming and cool. Aimee, in a turquoise bikini, inches in, her arms waving in the air, her face scrunched up. "Oh my god, it's freezing," she squeals to her friends. Her nipples pop under the thin fabric of her top. She crosses her arms over her chest. Natasha, her friend, sits on a rock, holding her knees. "You coming, or what?" Aimee calls out to her.

I swim to a rock in the middle of the river and back, happy Aimee is too occupied to notice me. Dawn struts toward the river. Her curls are wild, like the mosh pit in a Nirvana video. She flips them over to one side to keep them out of her eyes while she pokes in a toe. "Damn, Marisa, that's cold," she says, noticing me.

"Swim and you'll warm up," I yell back.

"Yeah, did you hear that, Natasha? Swim!" Aimee shouts, still inching her way in.

Dawn holds her hands on her hips. She's wearing long swim trunks and a surf top. Her chest is flat. Aimee's chest is round, bulging out of her bikini top.

"Oh, nice bathing suit, Dawn. Really shows off your curves," Aimee taunts, her lips widening into a snake-like grin.

Dawn ignores her and wades in close to me as Aimee watches.

Jean-Paul, our guide and lifeguard, is talking to some of the other girls who buzz nervously around him with their arms hugging their waists, but his eyes are on us swimmers.

Dawn dunks her head in the water and swims out a few feet away. Her curls are weighed down in front of her face. She spits out a stream of water. I laugh and do the same. Our attention is diverted when someone screams.

"Get your butt in here," Aimee calls as she pushes people out of her way, like a shark stalking through a kelp forest. She reaches Natasha and drags her friend into the water. Natasha resists, and it doesn't seem playful. Aimee's leg and ab muscles tighten, showing her strength over Natasha, whose legs jiggle with flab. My own legs are strong, but not as toned as Aimee's and with more cellulite. Aimee makes me self-conscious about stupid things like leg fat, and I instinctively pull at my tight swim shorts to cover my inner thighs.

"No, no, no Aimee, *pleeeeease*," Natasha pleads.

Her scream is cut off when Aimee over-powers Natasha and drags her into the river. She dunks Natasha's head into the water. When Natasha's head pops back up, her eyes are wide and she's gasping. Coughing.

Jean Paul blows his whistle. "No!" Natasha says again, and Aimee dunks her a second time.

Dawn and I swim closer. Dawn grabs Aimee around the waist and flips her over into the water, forcing her to let go of Natasha. We're in the shallows, but Natasha flails her arms and legs, gasping for air. I support Natasha under her arms and lift her up. Jean-Paul runs toward us. The girls surrounding him scatter to let him pass, like a pile of leaves blown by the wind, and he's next to us in no time.

"Slow down," I tell Natasha. "You can touch the bottom. Just breathe," I say, trying to calm her down. She finally hears me and takes in two short, shallow breaths, coughs, and breathes normally again.

Jean-Paul reprimands Aimee for roughhousing, but he doesn't sound too upset. His whistle is in one hand, and kickboard in the other. He flexes his arms and abs as he talks.

Aimee stands closer to him, her hands on her hips. "It was just a joke," she says.

Natasha takes a deep breath with her hand to her chest and walks to shore on shaky legs. "Thanks," she manages, as I lead her back.

Jean Paul turns to Aimee. "There is no play fighting in the water. No pushing or dunking. Is that clear?"

"Got it, thanks," Aimee says. When Jean Paul heads back to the group of girls, Aimee turns to Dawn. "I can't believe you touched me, freak."

"What the hell is your problem?" Dawn says to Aimee.

Natasha sits on a rock, holding her knees and shivering.

I've never stood up to Aimee, but with Dawn here, it seems easier. "That was really nasty," I say to Aimee, while handing Natasha my towel. She wraps it around herself. She's shaking so hard, I rub her back to warm her. She doesn't seem to mind, but I stop, thinking Aimee might get the wrong idea.

"Who asked you? We were having fun until you two got involved." Aimee's voice carries on the water and echoes on the mountains across the river.

"She couldn't breathe," I yell.

"Mind your own business!" Aimee says. "Natasha, show them you're fine."

Natasha wipes something off her rock. "M-maybe you sh-should bunk somewhere else."

Aimee's face changes—her grin is gone. "Tonight?"

"And after tonight," Natasha says, sitting up.

I'm not up to speed on what's going on between them, but Aimee's eyes tighten. She clears her throat and crosses her arms. "Fine. I'm sorry. Just chill."

I can't believe Aimee has just apologized for something.

She looks over her shoulder and mutters, "Crap. It's Mr. Belisle." Our teacher marches down the beach toward us. "Not a word or you're next," Aimee warns me, "and I won't let you up for air." I believe her.

"Everything okay, ladies?" Mr. Belisle asks. His beer belly sticks out of his too-tight Montreal Alouettes football T-shirt.

Natasha wraps my towel around herself tightly.

"Natasha, everything all right?" he asks, pointedly.

Aimee widens her eyes at Natasha and shakes her head.

"Yeah, the water is just cold," Natasha says, her voice and body shaking.

Dawn is next to me and shouts, "That's bull! Aimee was drowning her."

"Ms. Morosa, that's a serious allegation."

"I warned them about roughhousing near water. It can be dangerous. No more, please," Jean-Paul says.

Fists clenched at her sides, Dawn looks like she might slug our guide for downplaying the whole thing.

"Sorry, Mr. B. Won't happen again," Aimee says. "Thank you, *Ms. Morosa*, but all's good here." Aimee snorts and wraps her arm around Natasha, who stands up and moves away.

Dawn pounds her fist on her hip. I tap her shoulder, and she relaxes a little.

"Let's just go," I say, gritting my teeth. I don't ask for my towel back.

CHAPTER NINE

Sparks

Natasha may not be able to swim, but she can pitch a tent in no time. Good thing for Aimee, Natasha somehow forgave her and was willing to share her tent after all. We're supposed to set up around the fire pit, but I've got my tent a little farther away from the glow of the surrounding torch lights. I don't want Aimee watching my every move.

Everyone is tinkering with their equipment, and it's quiet, except for the sound of the wind in the trees around the clearing. It's not a wide area, but large enough for the twenty of us to set up.

A few boys across from me laugh and banter, trying to make up for the trouble they're having with their pop-up tent. I can't untie the rope around my sleeping bag, so I use the Swiss Army knife to cut through it. With one flick of my wrist, the rope pops off. I can tie the ends up again when I have to roll up my bag. I set the knife down and lay my sleeping bag in my tent. I've forgotten to secure my tent, and search my bag for the pegs, but can't find them. I empty it out, hoping I haven't forgotten them.

"Need these?" It's Aimee, bending down, still in her bikini top, and I think she might spill out of it. She holds my four yellow pegs in her hands. Natasha and two other girls are with her.

"Yeah, thanks," I say, sure to look her in the eye and not at her chest.

She whisks them away from me and leans closer. "I see the way you look at me, L'Heureux. Don't have any wet dreams about me and come sniffing around my tent tonight." She holds up the pegs and drops them, then walks away with her friends.

I hammer the pegs into the ground, picturing Aimee's face with each strike.

If it wasn't for Aimee and her toxicity, I'd love it here. There are no trucks speeding by or tractors rumbling, like on my country road at home. There is no air or light pollution from the factories in town. When the stars come out, it'll be spectacular. For the next half hour, I sit in my tent and enjoy the sky through the netted ceiling.

I sit up when I hear Jean-Paul having trouble starting the campfire. Aimee watches over him, her hand on his shoulder. She kneels next to him, blowing on the logs. The wood has been smoking for the last half hour, and still no flame. He's too distracted to notice, but the logs are probably too humid. And he's got them lying on top of each other with no way for air to pass. *How did this guy end up being our nature guide?* I want to grab the logs and set them up, platform style like a pyramid, but I'm not about to interrupt the sparks flying between him and Aimee. I lie back down and mind my own business.

CHAPTER TEN

Ripped at the Seams

My attention is diverted from the fire when I hear Dawn swear from across the clearing.

"Need a hand?" I call out.

Aimee whips her head away from Jean-Paul like a great white smelling the blood of its prey.

"My tent is ripped," Dawn yells back, holding a limp tarp in her hands.

"How bad is it? I've got duct tape," I say. She brings it to me and there's a gash in the side, beyond repair. I laugh.

"This is funny?" Dawn smiles and drops the tent.

"Sorry. You think you'd have noticed the gash, though." It is long and straight, not a rough tear, and looks like it's been sliced on purpose. "You can bunk with me." The offer just comes out, like I would do if Rock needed help.

"Really? You think we're allowed?"

I shrug. "Everyone else is bunking," I say, pointing to the boys across from us. She doesn't answer right away. *Is she worried about bunking with me?* My parents, in their infinite wisdom, wrote to my teachers after I came out to give them a *head's up* about my *situation* and to keep an eye out for me—whatever that means. Now everyone knows. Mr. Belisle might not be comfortable with us sharing a tent; he just doesn't get it, and I'm not about to ask permission and get into the whole gender and sexual identity discussion at survival camp. That's the type of survival I have to do every single day—and maybe Dawn does, too.

"Lights out at midnight, kids!" Mr. Belisle says. He slips on the band of his headphones, adjusts them, holds the ear cups, and then bobs his head to the music as he crawls into his tent. Dawn accepts my offer and opens her sleeping bag in my tent, and we settle in.

I wasn't nervous with Dawn on the bus, but now, in this tiny space, I'm afraid I might talk in my sleep or fart, or do something weird. We listen in silence to the other campers chat and laugh by the fire Jean-Paul has finally started. Sweet smoky maple wood cuts the humid air.

"You and Rock are good friends," Dawn says out of nowhere.

"Since forever."

"He seems nice."

At school, Dawn's usually alone, nose in a book. "You can hang out with us, whenever you like," I say. "It would be fine with him."

"I don't want to be in anyone's way."

"No problem, so long as you don't mind being treated like slug mucus by Aimee and her troupe."

"I've already checked that one off my list," Dawn says.

We both laugh, and afterward, we have nothing left to say. Dawn loops a curl around her finger, and I twist a loose thread from my sleeping bag around mine. Crickets sing and there's a light breeze making a swishing sound in the trees. Water laps up against the rocks onshore. It's only ten-thirty.

"You tired?" I ask.

"Sort of," Dawn says. "But can I ask you something? Kind of personal?"

I get cold and sweaty at the same time. "Sure."

"You're gay, right?"

"Yeah," I answer uncertainly, worrying about where this is going. This question is usually followed by raised eyebrows, or by me watching straight girls walk away because they think we can't be friends. I think Dawn and I could be friends, but if this is going to get weird now, I'll regret asking her to share my tent. I swear, if finding myself in awkward situations could be a superpower, I'd rule the world.

"So, you only like girls?" The word "only" throws me off. I look up at the starry sky through the mesh ceiling of our tent.

"I've never liked a guy," I say, honestly.

"Oh."

"Are *you* gay?" I ask. Dawn doesn't answer. She twists in her sleeping bag to look at the sky.

"Crap. I'm sorry. I didn't mean to put you on the spot. You don't have to answer that; I'm just . . ."

But before I can think of how to make this any less weird, Dawn says with glistening eyes, "Would you like me if I was?"

"I like you now," I say honestly.

There's a loud, long hooting. Wings flap, and I imagine a loon skittering across the water. A moment later, a second loon answers, its yodel echoing back. Dawn is smiling, and I'm a whole new kind of sweaty.

"Yeah?" she says. "Not many people do."

"You're cool and smart, and funny, and honest. Most people don't know how to deal with that."

"Thanks," Dawn says.

The campfire crackles, and I imagine the sparks waving into the air as we enjoy the stars. We chat a little more, mostly about school, until a loud snort jolts me. I kneel and look out the top of our tent, and a light shines on my face.

CHAPTER ELEVEN
Intrusion

"Were you two kissing?" Aimee squeals. She hunches down to poke her head through my tent flap; her cell phone pointed at me. "I think this sort of thing is frowned upon," she adds.

Of course, Aimee has to barge in on us and make everything painfully awkward. Dawn shields her eyes with her hand to block the light.

"Get the hell out," I say, and throw my backpack at her. Big mistake. Aimee catches and unzips it. She rifles through my stuff, grabbing at everything.

"Nice supplies. Looks like this will come in handy on a hike. Compass, matches? It looks like you have everything," she says. "Or do you?"

I pull my bag away from her and sift through the pockets. I can't find my Swiss Army knife. "Give it back!" I'm about to push her out of my tent, but Aimee jerks back.

"*Shhh*," Aimee hisses. "Keep your voice down. You don't want Mr. Belisle to know what was happening here, right?" She points between me and Dawn.

"You took my knife," I say.

"Why would I do that?" she asks. "And why would you have one to begin with?"

I'm suddenly transported in memory to the last time I had to use the knife—the day of my test flight when I cut through my seatbelt.

"What's going on?" Mr. Belisle's voice breaks through my thoughts. His headphones are curled around his neck. He's waiting for me to answer. I must look terrible because his face softens. "Marisa, do you feel all right?"

"She was complaining of menstrual cramps earlier so I came to check on her, Mr. B," Aimee lies.

"Oh." He clears his throat and fidgets with his earphones. "Is that all?"

"I'm fine, Mr. Belisle, really," I say, because I want him out of my tent.

"You two are bunking together?" he asks, noticing Dawn in her sleeping bag.

"Her tent was torn," I say, giving Aimee an accusatory side eye, "so I invited her to stay with me."

Aimee snorts, then clears her throat when Mr. Belisle looks at her.

"You should have asked permission," he says.

"Aimee and Natasha are bunking together. So are some of the boys," Dawn says.

"Yes, but . . ." he hesitates, "that's different."

My mouth drops open. My armpits are sweaty. My cheeks flush. I inhale through my nose, trying to find something to say, but Dawn beats me to it.

"Sir, that's an extremely insensitive assumption. We're friends. Marisa helped me out. We were just talking."

"Didn't look that way." Aimee waves her cell phone at me from behind Mr. Belisle's back.

"Maybe you should mind your own business," Dawn says to Aimee.

"Okay, let's just calm down. Aimee, you came to check on Marisa. She's fine. Go back to your tent. Ladies," he pauses, "lights out at midnight."

"Yes, O Captain! My Captain!" Dawn salutes him.

"Don't push it, Morosa," he says, leaving our tent. Finally.

"That was awesome," I tell her.

"Why is it so hard to tell on Aimee?" Dawn asks.

"Because it'll make things worse. Besides, I think she stole my knife and I don't need her blabbing about it." I turn on my flashlight and set it in the corner.

"And why do you have it, anyway?"

"Basic survival gear. Besides, Aimee has it now."

"Do you think . . ." she trails off, then starts again. "Do you think Aimee cut my tent?" she asks.

"Definitely,"

"She sucks."

I can't help smiling.

"But I'm kind of glad I don't have to bunk alone," Dawn says.

"Why's that?"

"I don't know. It's really dark out here. Lots of strange noises."

I cannot believe Dawn is telling me she's afraid of the dark.

"And you seem to know your way around a campsite."

"And who wants to face Aimee alone?" I say.

"Exactly." Dawn looks up at the stars. "Thanks for letting me bunk with you." She glances at me. Her eyeliner is smudged and dark around her eyes. "You're smart," she says. "You're the kind of person I should team up with on a nature hike."

"Could be cool if we were paired together," I say.

Dimples appear on Dawn's cheeks. Her hair is frizzy from humidity. Her lips are full. She's really pretty.

"You're smart, too," I say. "The way you spoke to Mr. Belisle."

"Well, *thaaaank* you *daaarling*!" Dawn says in an exaggerated and terrible British accent. She waves like the queen and primps her hair.

I burst out laughing.

"*Shhhh*," Dawn whispers. "Don't want Mr. Belisle to come back. The vein in his neck was about to pop when he saw me here. Like one move and he'd turn into the Hulk. A homophobic, heavy-metal loving Hulk."

I crack up even more, and Dawn joins in.

Across the clearing, Mr. Belisle yells, "Quiet over there!"

"We're two *brainiacs*, I guess," I whisper.

"Yeah. Failing school and begging for credits to pass. If I don't get my credits, my parents are definitely forcing me to do summer school," Dawn says. "You?"

"Same. And I won't be allowed to continue my cadets training."

"Cadets? Cool."

We're quiet for a few minutes. We should rest for tomorrow, but I want to keep talking to Dawn. She's fun and interesting and I want to know more about her, but I'm not ready to get into everything with the test flight, so I don't mention cadets again.

Dawn speaks first. "I'd love to hang out with you and Rock. Thanks," she says, biting her lower lip.

I'm smiling a wide, goofy smile, I know it, so I cover my face. It's not so bad without Rock here. Dawn is fun. But I'll bet Aimee will ruin everything. She always does.

CHAPTER TWELVE

S.O.S

It's getting late, but we chat a little more, mostly about school. She talks about her band that sucks because no one really knows how to play their instruments. She has her brother's old bass guitar, but she can't afford lessons. She's trying to teach herself, but it's not going so well. Her band is called Lazy Squirrels, and I want to ask about where the name came from, but Dawn is into telling me about the songs they're trying to cover. It's mostly punk rock and alternative, but she really likes jazz, too.

"Jazz is so smooth and comforting. Like hot chocolate," she says, yawning. "I'm wilting here. I think I'm ready to turn out the lights."

"Yeah, we should get some sleep," I agree.

She clicks her flashlight off and in a few moments, she's breathing loudly and slowly.

I wish I could fall asleep as easily, but I keep thinking about Aimee with my knife. She might tell Mr. Belisle about it, or plant it somewhere to make me look like some psycho.

If I get caught, Mr. Belisle might kick me out of camp, and call my mom to come get me. That would be a nightmare, a total embarrassment, but then at least I wouldn't have to deal with Aimee for the next few days. There is only one bar on my cell phone, but I roll over and text Rock: "**S.O.S.**"

After ten minutes, he still has not responded, and I don't know why I ever decided to come on this trip without him. I'm no match for Aimee. My heart is beating fast, and I try to catch my breath, but it's out of reach. I wheeze and gasp. I'm crash landing, again. The next thing I know, Dawn is next to me, her flashlight on.

"Breathe, Marisa," she says, her eyes tired and puffy, but wide too, afraid. For me.

"I'm . . ." I try again to catch my breath. "I'm okay," I whisper, and lie back down.

"What's happening?" she asks.

"Bad dream," I lie. The nightmare is real. The memory of sinking a few hundred feet in the air through turbulence has me spinning. Dawn waits for me to catch my breath.

"You're worried about Aimee. And the knife?"

"It's stupid."

"No, it's not. She's horrible."

"It's not just her. I mean the knife, it . . ." I don't know how to express what I feel about a stupid, little object I want back so badly.

"Mr. Belisle will understand. It *is* pretty basic camping gear, like you said. I don't think it's a big deal."

"Right," I say, trying to hide how I really feel.

"Is it sentimental or something? You're upset about losing it?"

That's it. That's exactly it. How did she know? "Yeah," I say.

"Okay, so we'll get it back. Somehow. Tomorrow. But tonight, I think we need to sleep or we'll be total wrecks for the hike." She reaches her hand over to touch my sleeping bag. "Okay?"

"Yeah. Sorry to wake you. I'm fine."

She rolls over and falls asleep again quickly. I hold my phone under my pillow, but Rock never texts me back. I finally fall asleep and when I open my eyes again, the sky is still dark, a streak of light blue hitting the horizon beyond the river.

CHAPTER THIRTEEN

Wet Granola Bars and Tampons

The sun comes up with blue jays squawking in the trees. Footsteps approach nearby and soon Jean-Paul is at our tent, shouting, "Rise and shine. Get your stuff and meet me at the fire pit, packed and ready for action."

His cheeriness makes me want to throw my backpack at him, but I can't find it. Dawn stretches, then yawns. "Hey. Morning."

"Time to get set," I say, punching the air with fake enthusiasm.

"I hope we can partner up for the hike. I mean, if you want to," Dawn says, still yawning.

"Sure," I say, searching for my bag. "Is my bag on your side?"

Dawn rolls around and pulls off her sleeping bag to check, but my backpack isn't in the tent. "I don't see mine either," she says.

I check my phone. No reception and no text from Rock. "Damn it." I pull open the flap to the tent. Mosquitoes are already on the attack when I trip over my bag. I know I didn't leave it here. When I pick it up, it's heavier than I remember, and when I hold the bottom for support, I know why. It's sopping wet.

"Three guesses who did that, and the first two don't count," Dawn says, eyeing my bag.

"What about you? Did she get to yours?" I ask.

"It looks dry." She pulls hard to pick it up, but it's lighter than she expects, and she hits herself in the face with it.

She didn't appreciate me laughing at her ripped tent yesterday, so I hold back. "She took your stuff?" I ask.

"It's not empty," Dawn says, unzipping her bag. She sets it down and reaches inside to pull out what looks like packing peanuts.

"What is that?"

Dawn doesn't answer but laughs instead. It's a nasal giggle at first, but then it bubbles into a whole-hearted, stomach-achy, uncontrollable laugh. I close in to see inside her bag—it's filled with tampons.

"She's so horrible," I say, wishing I could let things roll off my shoulders like Dawn does. "This doesn't bother you?"

She throws the tampons into the air, like confetti. "Whatever. I don't need these. I hope she gets her period during the hike. Better pick them up, though, before any animals chew them up." Dawn stuffs the tampons back into her bag. "At least she left my water and food." Dawn grabs a bunch of tampons and dumps them into my hands. "Here. You never know."

I take them, matching Dawn's smile because it's contagious and bright, and find a dry compartment in the back pocket of my bag.

All my equipment is here, but not my knife. My compass still works, but the matches are wet and useless, and my two water bottles are gone. I remember Jean-Paul's instructions about the toilets, and how there is no running water on site. I take a walk around the campsite, and near the bathrooms are two large recycling bins. I look around to be sure no one is watching and pull out three empty plastic water bottles. I give them a wipe and, satisfied, pack them in my bag.

"Rifling through trash?" Aimee says to me on her way to a toilet.

I don't have any quick remarks, and even if I did, she would probably have an answer for it, so I ignore her and walk back to my tent.

After a quick breakfast of oddly satisfying wet granola bars, Dawn and I meet the others at the fire pit.

"Finally," Jean-Paul says when we arrive, Aimee walking behind us. "I'm matching you with your hike buddies." He flips a page on his clipboard. Dawn inches closer to me. I can feel her warm breath on my neck and her hand brushing up against my elbow. It's like walking into spider webs: tingly, but soft. It's a little scary, but only until you realize the thing you walked into is actually nature's work of art.

Dawn's fingers flutter at mine, and it feels like sparkles. I turn to Dawn and smile, but Jean-Paul's words puncture through our moment.

"Marisa, Aimee, and Dawn. Get your gear. Pick up your maps and supplies."

I suppress a groan. Aimee rolls her eyes at me. Dawn smiles. How can she look so happy? This is going to be a nightmare.

For the next hour, Jean-Paul shows us how to read a topographic map to know where the trails will lead us uphill. The park is huge. The trails dip and climb through the mountains. I read the map carefully and note an emergency medical cabin on-site near a bridge in the centre of the park. It's just around a bend in the river where the seaplane landed yesterday. Aimee isn't even looking at the map, but hiding her phone in her lap and texting. As Chris Hadfield says in his book, *you'll feel confident if you know how to work through a problem*. Right now, my problem is dealing with Aimee as a hiking partner.

Jean-Paul continues our survival lesson by teaching us how to use a compass, as well as our satellite communicators. Basic stuff. To everyone's disappointment, we have to swap our cell phones for a communicator. It's like a small walkie-talkie with an S.O.S feature that will send Jean-Paul our GPS coordinates in case we get lost.

He warns us to use the designated rest spots for eating as they are equipped with locking garbage bins to be sure raccoons, bears, and other wildlife are not attracted to our food. "In case you do encounter any wildlife," he says, "walk away. Slowly. If you encounter a bear, do not run. Don't scream or yell, but make noise. Talk, or sing."

"Sing?" Dawn asks.

"Yeah," I tell her. "Let it know you're not a threat. In cadets, they suggested we sing 'Happy Birthday' because it has a calm, monotone melody and everyone knows the words."

"The sound of me singing might be enough for it to attack. I'll leave the singing to you," she says.

"Girls. You listening?" Jean-Paul picks on us.

"Yeah, sorry," I say.

"But Marisa is right. Singing a monotone song can be calming for everyone. You've been trained well, Marisa. You're in good hands," he says to Aimee and Dawn.

"Thanks."

"*Ew,*" Aimee says from behind me. "Hands off, L'Heureux.

"So. Stay calm. Walk away," Jean-Paul says.

Sounds like the right advice on how to deal with Aimee, too.

"And communicate your location," he continues. The students buzz with questions, but Jean-Paul repeats the simple directions. It reminds me a lot of *Aviate, Navigate, Communicate.* Work the problem, as Chris Hadfield says.

Everything Jean-Paul shows us is stuff I've already learned with cadets, but it's good to have a refresher. Aimee smiles and nods like a puppet at everything Jean-Paul says, but I doubt she's actually paying attention.

When our info session is done, Aimee eyes me over her shoulder and hoists her heavy bag onto her back. "What are you staring at? I'm not into threesomes. Get your stuff and let's go," she barks at me and Dawn.

I don't dare tell her she'll regret the extra weight, but I know it'll slow us down.

CHAPTER FOURTEEN

Take a Hike

"Okay, so we have to go up the ridge, cross a bridge, and follow the trail back to camp around the spot we swam in yesterday. The map says ten kilometers. How long will that take?" Dawn asks, reading her map.

"At this pace, all day and night," Aimee says, folding up her own map.

"A couple of hours, depending on how much climbing we have to do," I answer. "We'll have to keep moving to make it back to camp by three o'clock." It's not a race, but if we're not back in time, we don't get our credits. We each pack our bags.

"What about lunch?" Aimee asks. "You can afford to skip a meal, but I can't."

We're allowed a few liters of water, but we're not given any food since we were expected to pack our own. Aimee scans me, and I'm ultra-aware of my thighs rubbing against each other. I pack my things, trying to ignore Aimee, like Dawn does.

"Bring snacks," I tell her, thinking of the soggy peanut butter sandwich and two granola bars in my pack.

Dawn packs her water bottles and offers me one. "Keep them," I say, and am sure to bring my empty bottles along. I use a pen to pierce a few holes at the bottom of one of the bottles. If I had my knife, this would be a lot easier. I borrow a pair of scissors from Jean-Paul and cut the second bottle in half, but keep both pieces.

"Smart," he says, as I give him the scissors back. "I have purification tablets I can give you for the water," he offers.

"I have what I need, thanks," I say, but double check my bag to be sure Aimee didn't lift them when she rifled through my bag last night. The sealed pack is in my bag and the tablets are intact.

"Always prepared?" he asks.

"Almost always," I say, wishing I had my knife.

"What's with the arts and crafts?" Aimee asks, pointing at the bottle.

"She's preparing a water filter," Jean-Paul says. "Looks like you've got a real survivalist on your team," he adds.

"Great. Well, at least *I* came prepared," Aimee says, then slurps from her canteen. I want to rant about my spilled water, but her thin-lipped smile tells me there's no point. Jean-Paul leaves to check on the other groups, and Aimee opens her bag. I can see she's carrying more than the four liters of water we're allowed. By the size of her bag, I'd say Aimee is carrying at least two more bottles. If Aimee is caught cheating, she won't get her credits. If I'm caught knowing she was cheating, neither will I. I should tell Mr. Belisle, but she'll bring up my knife if I say anything about her extra water.

I'd love to ditch Aimee and complete this hike alone with Dawn, but Jean-Paul and Mr. Belisle were clear about the rules: In order to get our credits, we must complete the hike with our assigned partners. No credits, no graduation. No test flight. But I can't think about flying right now, so I put the thought aside. *Work the problem.* I should only worry about the hike.

"I'm ready. Let's go, already," Aimee complains.

"It's this way," I say to Aimee, who's headed in the wrong direction. I show her the rest spots marked on the map, and review our designated path, which is different for each team.

"You should have space for this," I say, handing her the communicator. If Dawn or I keep it, Aimee will try to take it anyway, or blame us if something happens to it. If she has it, she's responsible for it. I give it to Aimee. She places it into her bulging bag.

"Okay. Ready," she says again, slinging her bag over her shoulder. It's bright red with blue hearts on it. It's torn in a few places, like she's had it forever. She holds the straps, fidgeting with the loose ends, and for a second, she looks unsure of herself, like a kid on the first day of school. But the image rolls away quickly when she says, "Get your fat asses moving! I want to be back before sundown."

It's uphill at the start of our hike. That's a good thing since our energy is high now. But after only half an hour, the humidity makes me sweaty and sticky, which means I need to drink, even if I'm not thirsty. The land levels off and there is a stream passing through a shady spot where we stop to catch our breath. Aimee stops ahead of me and pulls out her bottle taking one, two, three huge gulps.

"Save your water," I say.

"I'm not sharing," she says.

"I'm not asking, but if you drink it all and have nothing left, you'll get dehydrated quickly."

"It'll get really hot this afternoon. Save your water," Dawn adds.

"But I'm thirsty now," Aimee says. She scratches her arm. Under her sleeve, I notice a disk stuck to her skin. A nicotine patch? Contraceptive patch? I don't have enough time to analyze it and she notices me watching her. "I've got more water, okay. Quit nagging."

I take out my empty bottle from my backpack, stuff a piece of fabric from the bottom of my bag into it, and add rocks from the stream. I fill the rest of the bottle with water. I place it inside the half-cut bottle so filtered water can drip into it. I place it in the netting on the side of the bag so it won't leak. There should be enough to drink in about fifteen minutes.

"*Ew*," Aimee says. "What are you supposed to do with that?"

"It's a water filter," Dawn answers for me. "So cool." Her full lips stretch over her teeth. Her smile is wide and hopeful.

"Cadets," I say.

"Nice. I used to be a girl scout, but I quit when I was seven. Can you drink it like that?" she asks.

"It needs to be filtered, then purified with tablets to get rid of bacteria. Then, yeah, I can just drink it."

"It looks like mud," Aimee says.

"It'll be fine," I tell her. "I don't have much choice," I add.

"You can have some of mine in the meantime." Dawn unscrews the cap of her bottle and hands it to me.

I know I can hold out longer. During our cadets' training, we were on a similar hike, except without the deep canopy of treetops to keep us shaded and cool. I held off drinking and made it back to training camp soaked and exhausted, dizzy and nauseous with heatstroke. Commander Hensen insisted on having me strapped to an I.V. for twenty-four hours to stay hydrated, but I was fine. So, I can wait a little longer, but Dawn is holding her bottle toward me expectantly.

"I have enough," she insists.

"Just drink it, already," Aimee says.

I take a small sip, conserving Dawn's water. She takes her bottle back and her eyes are bright. "Much better," I say. "Thanks so much."

"Anytime," Dawn says, putting her bottle away without looking away from me.

"Oh geez. Don't you two get all homo on me. Hurry up," she orders, and we continue uphill to where the path finally plateaus.

In the distance, thunder grumbles. It's mild at first, then louder, echoing through the park, like an angry monster coming to life.

CHAPTER FIFTEEN

A Thorn in the Lion's Paw

"Looks like the rain will hold off for a little while, but check this out," I say, pointing out from the top of the ridge. We can see the entire forest from here. Tips of pine trees poke the skyline above the mountains, and there is a fresh smell of wet rock in the air. A waterfall roars behind the wall of trees. To our right is a rickety wooden staircase leading to a platform above the trees where we can get a better look. I test the first step, and it doesn't crumble, so I walk up gently.

"It's a detour. We should keep going," Aimee says, wiping sweat from her brow. "We want to be back in time, remember?"

"It'll take ten seconds and we'll have a better view of the falls," I say, beginning to climb the steps.

"Running water. Big whoop."

Dawn ignores Aimee and climbs with me to the top. It's only about fifty steps, but higher ground allows us the perfect view of a white waterfall cascading across the rocks, plummeting downstream. A bridge runs across the peak of the falls, and when I check the map, it's confirmed this is where we're headed. I point it out to Aimee, but she's unresponsive. Ignoring me, she grips the guardrail with white knuckles. She's looking a little green.

"You okay?" I ask. "You afraid of heights?"

"No way," she scoffs. "We're wasting time." She's a bad liar.

It's only 9:30 a.m. and we have more than enough time to complete the hike, but Aimee is in a constant rush. I think I hear thunder again, but it's my stomach grumbling. It's too early for lunch, so I check on my water.

In my bottle, the filtered stream water is still a little cloudy, but there are no more particles floating around. Water fills the bottom part of my filter. I carefully pour it back into another empty bottle and find the tablets in my bag, then pop one into the water and shake it.

"Wait. You're not going to get crazy diarrhea or something from drinking that, are you? I need to finish this hike."

"The tablet will work. I'll have purified water in about half an hour," I say, shaking the bottle in front of her. But before I can put the bottle back in my pouch, she's knocked it out of my hand, over the railing, and it bounces on a few rocks before disappearing.

"What's your problem?" I hold out my hands, unable to catch my bottle, ready to wring her stupid neck. "Seriously. All of it. The pushing around into the lockers, soaking my bag." I pull it off my shoulders and whip it at her chest. "And now this. What is it about me that makes you a total bitch?" Dawn is next to me, and it's as though she's given me this confidence to speak to Aimee like I never have before.

Aimee drops my bag at my feet, opens her own, and hands me a transparent water bottle. "Don't be so dramatic. Here. Drink. I don't want you getting sick on my watch."

"My water was fine."

"Yeah, yeah, you're all survival savvy and stuff. Doesn't mean you have to drink mud. Just take it."

For a second, I think it might be poisoned and I hesitate. She unscrews the top of her canteen and drinks, rolling her hand around to show me I should do the same.

I take a small sip; it's cool and fresh. I'm tempted to chug the whole thing, but limit myself to one more sip. Aimee stuffs her bottle back into her bag, and when I catch a glimpse inside, there's loads of stuff including shoes and clothes she doesn't need for the hike.

"Thanks," I say. I pick up my bag and keep the bottle she gave me in my side pocket. Aimee doesn't respond.

"You have extra water," Dawn says, also noticing the contents of Aimee's bag. "Why would you risk cheating and getting caught if you're so set on finishing this hike?"

"You two worry a lot. You should worry more about—"

I've had enough. I cut her off. "What? My fat ass? My heavy thighs? Any other great advice?"

She supports the bottom of her bag with one hand and tightens one strap with the other. "I was going to say your wet mop attitude." Her hand waves in front of my face and I swat at it.

"What is your problem?" I ask again.

"No problem, sunshine. I just don't like you." She looks at Dawn. "Deal with it." She makes her way back down the steps.

"So, you treat us like garbage? Why?" I push past her. "If you don't want to do this with us, just take off!"

"I can't, remember? I'm stuck with you."

"And why is that so terrible?" I ask.

"You're just, so . . ."

"What?"

"Clueless. You have it easy with your outdoorsy skills and . . . " She takes a step back. Looks me up and down. "Everything else."

"*Everything* else?" I ask. "What does that mean? How is being paired with you easy for me?" I point at Aimee and wave my hand in her face. "And I learned the outdoor stuff. You can, too. Just pay attention."

"Do we *really* need to talk? Can't we just get through this hellish day and skip to the part where we jump in the river later?"

"We have to finish the hike first," Dawn says. "So let's calm down."

Thunder rolls across the hills again. "Perfect," Aimee says.

"Rain might not be so bad," I say. It might do us some good and help us cool off.

"Shut up and walk." Aimee pushes my shoulder slightly to hurry me along. I want to slug her but don't turn around until the steps shake with a loud thud. I almost laugh because Aimee's foot has smashed through a rotten plank. But, then I realize she's bleeding where a chunk of wood has punctured her skin. It doesn't look deep, but Aimee gets impatient and tries to pull her foot out of the hole as I assess the damage.

"Just a sec. It's not a good idea to pull it out too fast. The wood might be in deeper than you think," I say, but Aimee still twists her foot, trying to get it out. She almost loses her balance, and Dawn moves to support her from falling.

"Hands off, *lesbo*," she tells her, and snakes free from the hole. Blood trickles down her calf. Aimee's face is pale and sweaty, and I can tell the blood is making her nervous.

"Sit," I suggest. "I can pull it out or bandage it up. Let me look at it." She actually listens and sits. "It's not too deep. I can take it out, then clean out the wound. It might hurt, though," I tell her.

"Just do it," she says, her hands covering her face. Dawn's expression is of total shock—not at the blood, I don't think, because there really isn't much of it—but at how scared Aimee looks. She never looks scared.

I don't have gloves like I've been taught to wear when dealing with bleeding. I wipe my forehead with the sleeve of my T-shirt and rummage through Aimee's bag. I find two empty Ziploc bags. Good enough. They make a crinkling sound as I put them over my hands.

I tug at the splinter in Aimee's leg and she lets out a yelp, like a puppy whose tail has been stepped on. I make sure there isn't any wood stuck in the wound. Aimee's eyes are shut tight, and she's eerily quiet. She sits on the step and breathes heavily. I unscrew the cap on a water bottle and pour the clean water over her wound, making sure the splinter hasn't left behind any debris. Sweat is dripping from every crevice of my body, all hot and itchy. Then my Swiss Army knife pokes out of Aimee's shorts pocket. I slide it out and use it to cut a sleeve off a hoodie in her bag.

"Hey, my sweater," she protests.

"Forget it," I say, out of breath from the climb, the heat, and now this. "You don't want blood dripping everywhere." Aimee yields. The sleeve is long enough to tie around her calf. I could use it to soak up the blood, but it might get dirty and so will the wound. "I need something else to absorb the blood," I say to Dawn. "You have anything not too bulky?"

"Tampons!" Dawn shouts, like she's yelling an answer at a game show.

"Perfect," I say, and take them out of the pocket in my bag.

"I guess they're useful after all," Aimee says, like she's trying to make light of all this, but I can tell she's nervous as hell.

"Yeah, real practical. It'll do," I say. Dawn helps me unwrap five tampons. I gently pull off the plastic applicators and stick the cottony tampons in the sleeve, halfway through. I tie the sleeve around her leg, but not too tight.

"Attractive," Aimee says, assessing my handiwork. It's the closest I'll get to a *thank you* from her.

"You'll survive," I tell her, pulling off the Ziploc bags. I pocket my knife.

"Geez, I'm not diseased or anything, you could have done without those."

"It's Survival 101. And you're welcome, by the way."

She reaches for the ramp to get to her feet, but it's a bit wobbly. Again, Dawn offers her support, and this time, Aimee lets Dawn help. "Okay, I got it, you can stop trying to cop a feel," she says, steadying herself.

"You can quit it with the dumbass, homophobic comments, while you're at it," I say, as I collect the unused supplies. Then something beeps. At first, I think it's my watch, but we turned in all our devices.

"Is that the communicator?" I ask.

Aimee rolls up the bottom of her T-shirt. A small box is hooked to her belt.

"Shit," Aimee says, bending down to unzip a pouch on her bag. She pulls out her cell phone. Dawn watches, her face splotching with anger. Aimee reads what is probably a text from one of her many boyfriends and I roll my eyes.

"Seriously? Why are you even on this trip?" Dawn asks.

"Shut up for a second." Aimee taps her phone to the patch under her sleeve I noticed earlier. Her phone beeps again.

On her feet, Aimee picks up her shoe and hobbles down the steps. She's limping, but steady, and there's no blood dripping from the bandage. My confidence is up, and I follow my map toward the trail leading to the bridge and the waterfall. Another beep from behind me and Aimee is yelling.

"Hang on, I need a break," she says.

"But you were in such a rush to keep going," Dawn says.

I want to sit, too, catch my breath and eat something, but we've wasted quite a bit of time on the steps. I channel the mean spirit Aimee always lets loose, the one that keeps people from talking back to her. "You just had a break. Suck it up, princess," I say, almost convincingly.

"I need to rest," she insists. She's paler now than when she saw blood trickling from her leg, but I don't want to give in to her.

"You rest. We're walking," I say. I march on without Aimee. If Dawn follows me, great, but I don't know how much more Aimee I can take on this trip.

"You know, I didn't tell Mr. Belisle about your knife, but maybe I'll have a chat with him when we get back." The knife is secure, in my front pocket. I picture myself explaining to Mr. Belisle about the knife, how it's basic camping and survival gear. Maybe Jean-Paul will back me up, considering he saw me create my filter. I call her bluff.

"Whatever," I say, and continue to follow the trail, but Dawn pulls at my arm, holding me back.

"She doesn't look so good," Dawn says. "Like she might puke or faint." Dawn is right, but it's hard to believe. Aimee is a star athlete, and this mountain is taking a lot out of her. "It'll be harder to explain ditching Aimee than the knife. Let's take a break. I could use a rest, too." I'm calmed by Dawn's gentle tone.

"Okay. We'll walk until we find a spot to sit and eat." I pull out the map. "There's a rest spot in a few hundred meters. Can you make it?" I ask Aimee.

She gives me a thumb's up, then twists her hand into giving me the finger.

"Lovely." I follow the trail without looking behind to see if she's all right.

CHAPTER SIXTEEN

Kryptonite

Aimee is so slow. She should be strong enough to walk straight. Instead, she's dragging her feet and stumbling on rocks. She's probably doing it on purpose to piss me off.

"Seriously, Marisa, I need to eat something," Aimee whines, trailing behind me. She slipped up and used my actual name instead of *freak*, *loser*, or *dyke*. But my name in her voice sounds too personal. And it reminds me of when we were eight. And still friends. I'd ring her doorbell a few days a week and ask her to play. We'd climb fences and dig for treasure in a sandbox in her backyard. Then she started saying no when I asked her to play, and eventually, she stopped answering the door.

"We're almost there," I say.

I turn and she's holding her cell phone to the patch on her arm again, and it beeps like crazy. Her hand is shaking as she reads the screen.

"I need to stop now." She sits on a rock.

"We're only supposed to eat at the rest areas," I tell her.

"I don't see any bears," she says, and pulls out a handful of rolled-up something from one of the many compartments in her bag. The familiar sound of a candy wrapper crinkles. Now I know she's the one who's always eating candy in class.

"Rockets? Don't you have real food?" Dawn asks.

Aimee holds up a finger, telling us to wait and pops the whole roll of candy in her mouth and starts chewing, then opens the next one. She doesn't even offer us any.

Since Aimee gave me water, and I saved her from bleeding all over the trail, maybe she's feeling generous. I take a risk, and ask her, "Did you film us last night? In our tent?"

Her mouth is full. She pulls out her phone, and plays the video. The sound is muffled, and it's pretty dark. It's a crappy video with nothing to show.

"Why?" I ask.

"Figure I might catch you in the act or something."

"The *Act*?" I say. "We were talking."

"Nothing was going on." Dawn looks a little worried, I think, and I regret having brought this up now.

"Yeah. Pretty disappointing, overall," Aimee says. She shows me she is deleting the video. "Happy?"

"Even if something were going on, we wouldn't be ashamed." Dawn stands taller, but her cheeks are also splotchy again.

"Well, good for you. Be proud," Aimee says, but her words are thick with sarcasm. She's deleted the video, so I don't push the matter any further, even though I don't understand what her intentions were. I think I just stood up to Aimee. And it worked.

While Aimee eats another two rolls of candy, I indulge in a sip of water. Next, she takes out a healthy-looking protein bar. She's taking forever, but I'm patient. Dawn eats one of her snacks, too, and we huddle around the map and plan our way toward the bridge. It's getting hotter, so we move to a shady spot. There's thunder again in the distance, a little louder and closer than before. Aimee stands, holds her phone to her patch again, and it beeps, but only once. She reads her screen, looks satisfied, and packs up, ready to move.

"Okay. Go." Aimee points to the path.

We've lost precious time, but I'm too curious not to ask about her phone and the candy. "Explain first," I insist.

She shows me her screen. "Blood sugar was low. All good now."

"And that thing on your arm?" I ask.

"Blood sugar monitor. There's an app on my phone connected to it."

"The water and the cell phone; you weren't cheating? You're diabetic?"

Rolling her eyes, she mutters, "Great detective work."

"And when you looked like you were going to pass out? Was that because of low blood sugar?"

"Yeah. Whatever. I'm fine."

"You should have told us," Dawn says.

"None of your business."

"It is when you almost pass out and we have to stop every two minutes," Dawn argues.

"We had to stop because my leg went through rotten wood on a step *you two* insisted on climbing." She has a point there, so I get between them.

"We're here now. We should just continue."

"Because we all need our stupid credits, right?" Aimee untucks her shirt and lifts it. "You want to know everything, here you go." The skin on her stomach is smooth, and her abs are rippled, but I'm distracted by the tube and electronic device clipped to her shorts. "It's for insulin. A catheter. I have it permanently. Sometimes when I do physical activity, like a hike, or get stressed, like when I see blood, my sugar levels go down. If they go *way* down, this thing," she taps on the device, "blinks and beeps like crazy."

"Like your cell phone did?" Dawn asks.

"Yeah. But when my pump beeps," she taps the device again, "you need to shut off the stream of insulin by pressing this button twice. I'll probably be passed out by then, so radio for a helicopter transport or whatever."

"Seriously?" I ask.

"It's never happened before."

I wonder if this is why Mr. Belisle paired us together, knowing I've had survival training. It's not fair, stuck with Aimee because I'm well prepared. For a second, I think knowing her kryptonite might come in handy, but then I feel guilty, realizing she's been hooked up to this thing probably since . . .

"How long have you had the catheter?" I ask, letting her take my hand to help her stand. She lets go of me, suddenly, and sticks her hand in her pocket.

"I was nine. They put it in when they realized I would get super lazy and have no energy. My blood sugar would spike way up and this is the only way to control it, but it can go way down, too, so I have to check it, like, all the *friggin'* time. It's turned me into a bleeping machine."

Picturing Aimee on the basketball court, fast and lithe, I realize how much harder it must be with diabetes. She was diagnosed around the same time we stopped playing together. Maybe it had nothing to do with me, and everything to do with her being sick or trying to not be sick.

"Let's get going if we want to finish," Dawn reminds us.

Aimee's colour has come back, and she seems peppier. I'm reminded of the chocolate bar commercial: a person is really hungry and they're like The Hulk, until they eat a bar and they become super sweet. Maybe low blood sugar can explain Aimee's overall crappy attitude?

I doubt it.

Some things are stronger than blood.

Aimee's leg has stopped bleeding, so I guess that's one positive thing. She passes me on the trail as we head to the next rest stop.

The heat and humidity are pushing down on us, and it's getting late in the day. The sun is still high, but according to the map, we have more uphill climbing to do, steps to climb, and a bridge to cross. If we waste time, we won't make it, and there's no way I'm failing because of Aimee.

I've had no appetite since the blood and the arguing, but now my stomach is roaring louder than the waterfall and the thunder put together. I should eat, but we have to move. I'm drained from the heat, and from dealing with Aimee. But I trudge on.

CHAPTER SEVENTEEN

No Lifeguard on Duty

The waterfall is loud, which is good because it fills the awkward silence between the three of us. With Aimee's energy restored, we reach the bridge that crosses over the falls. It's no Niagara, but it's pretty. It's past one o'clock and we should pick up the pace, but it's hard not to admire the water cascading over the rocks. I watch the water rumbling below as we cross the bridge. The current splits around a small island downriver. There's a tree growing from a crack in the rock, which seems totally impossible. It's a muggy day, and the mist from the falls cools us.

Judging by the grey clouds, we might have rain for the second half of our hike. I don't love the idea of hiking in the mud, but anything would be better than this sweaty heat. We take a moment on the bridge to catch our breath and admire the view, but we have to keep moving.

We continue upriver, away from the falls. The L'Assomption river twists and turns in wide loops and we have to follow a long trail to another, smaller bridge which will lead us back to camp. We drag our feet in silence, the heat weighing us down. We don't stop until the trail leads far from the falls to a quiet, calm part of the river.

"Damn, it's hot," Dawn says, sipping water.

"We could cool off," Aimee suggests, pointing at the river water babbling over rocks. "Just wet our feet."

It would feel great to take a breather, and we've been making great time since the bridge, but I don't want to give into Aimee's suggestion.

"Hand me your map," Aimee says, holding out her hand.

"You have your own," I say.

"Just give," and she pulls it out of my back pocket, then opens it. "Check this out." I stand closer to her, but her hair is blocking the map, so I push it aside. She flinches. "Not so close," she says, and ties her hair in a high bun. She points to the map and I see what she sees. Our campsite is only about a kilometer from the trail on the opposite bank of the river. The water here looks shallow and calm. Cutting across would save us about an hour. It's not so much about making good time at this point, but we're drenched and tired and it would save us the trouble.

"No way," Dawn says, looking over my shoulder.

"Why not," Aimee says. "We could save loads of time, and cool off. Win-win."

"Unless we get caught. The other teams' trails meet with ours at some point, which means the other teams are not so far away, and if anyone sees us crossing, it might be considered cheating if we don't follow the path they've assigned us. And all this," Dawn waves an open hand at Aimee, "would be for nothing."

"Can we at least cool off? It's crazy hot."

"Who knows how powerful the current is," Dawn says.

"You're such a chicken shit," Aimee says.

"So be it. I need to graduate," Dawn says. "Marisa?"

I don't know what to say. Aimee is right—it would be so much easier. I think we can make it back to camp in the next few hours, but Dawn is also right—it's not worth the risk.

"We should follow the trail," I say.

"Sure, side with your girlfriend. *Boooooooring.*" But Aimee is already untying her shoes and pulling them off. She holds them both in one hand. "I'm going for it." She tugs at my T-shirt then grabs my arm, and I imagine this is what prey feels like when squeezed by a python.

I shake her free and refuse to follow. "Please don't take off, Aimee."

"See L'Heuruex, you do really like having me around."

I want to take it back. Part of me would love to have her gone, but as Dawn said, it would all be for nothing if we don't turn up together.

Aimee steps into the river, her shoes in hand. "So refreshing," she says, with her arms out for balance as she steps from one rock to the next

"If you arrive without us, Mr. Belisle will know you separated from us. We won't get our credits," I tell her. "And neither will you." She stops and considers what I'm saying.

"Relax, L'Heureux; just cooling off, like I said."

"I'm not following her," Dawn says, pointing to one of the many signs posted all around the area, with warnings like: *No lifeguard on Duty. Swimming is prohibited.* Obviously, Aimee doesn't care.

"Aimee, come on. Let's just finish this hike," I call out to her. I take a deep breath, ward off a shiver and say, "Together."

"Give me five minutes," she says, with her eyes on her feet as she steps through the water.

"The water is obviously off limits," Dawn says. "If Mr. Belisle happens by, or sees us from across the river, we'll be in trouble." I watch Aimee stretch out a long leg from rock to rock and her arms out for balance. The water looks cool and calm.

The humidity is suffocating, and a quick dip would feel great, but Dawn pulls me away by my sleeve. "Let's find a shady spot," she says.

"We'll wait for you in the shade, Aimee. Just make it quick." Aimee waves me off as I head back onto the trail.

The next moment, we hear Aimee swearing and calling us back. We ignore it until I detect panic and desperation in Aimee's *"Pleeeease!"*

CHAPTER EIGHTEEN

Slip Up

Aimee is sitting in the water, her butt totally submerged. She slips on the rocks every time she tries to stand.

"Great. What do we do now?" Dawn says. "I'm sick of wasting time on her."

"Marisa, I can't get up! It's too slippery." Aimee sounds panicked. And scared. She grunts as she tries again to stand and scrapes an elbow on one of the rocks.

"She's not joking, is she?" Dawn asks. Aimee looks genuinely terrified.

"Relax, Aimee. You're gonna hit your head or something," I call from the riverbank. She isn't too far out, not even halfway across the river, but I can tell she's frustrated. *What now?* "Let's work the problem." Chris Hadfield's words are all I can remember, but I'm not flying a plane. I'm trying to convince a stubborn bully to get out of the water she should have never stepped into. It's a million times harder than flying.

"What do I do now?" Aimee asks.

Work the problem. "You got there, so you can get back. Just relax. The water is only a few inches deep. The worst that can happen is a bad scrape. Get on your knees. Put one foot on a solid rock and stand. One step at a time back to shore."

She does as I say, and manages to stand. She wipes away sweat, maybe tears, too, and when she's upright I realize she doesn't have her pack on her back.

"Where's your bag?" I yell out.

"Shit," Dawn says from behind me. "Look." Aimee's bright-red backpack with hearts on it is bobbing in the water that pools around a few rocks. It is definitely soaked. Her food, water, and our communicator are all out of reach.

"We'll figure it out later. Let's just get you back to shore," I say.

Aimee takes short, careful steps, with her hands out at her sides. She stumbles a few times, but makes her way back to us. I hold out my hand to help her step onto shore without slipping. She takes it and makes it to shore red-faced and breathless—and empty handed.

"You lost your shoes, too?" Dawn asks, annoyed; her arms crossed.

"They fell in when I slipped and used my hands to break my fall," Aimee says. "I need my bag."

"We can do without it. I have a pair of flip-flops in my bag. Better than nothing," Dawn says, pulling them out.

Aimee slips them on without a *thank you*, her eyes glued to her bag.

"Forget it, Aimee," Dawn says. "You'll break your neck trying to get it. The rocks are too slippery."

"My insulin pump. It's in the bag."

"What? Why?" I ask.

"I didn't want it to get wet."

"Worked out perfectly," Dawn says.

I pull out my map. "Our trail intersects with the other teams in less than a kilometer. We're bound to run into someone with a communicator. We'll signal to Jean-Paul, if we need help. You seem to be feeling all right. Can you make it an hour or two without insulin?" I ask.

"I've never unhooked it for longer than half an hour, for showers and swimming."

"We have to keep going, then. Slow and steady. You've got this," I say, trying to sound encouraging. We have no choice but to continue. Dawn and I walk ahead and Aimee follows behind. I can't help but turn around to check on her every couple of minutes, but she seems to be doing okay.

"How are you so patient with her?" Dawn asks, with Aimee out of earshot.

I think of what Chris Hadfield says in his book about being a good leader. You don't have to be a superhero. Empathy and a sense of humour go a long way, but right now, nothing feels funny. "There's no point in losing my cool now. She knows she messed up. We need to get her back to camp. Diabetes can be serious if it's not monitored."

"You're good at this whole leadership thing," Dawn says.

"Cadets has taught me a lot."

"That's cool. Do you have, like, a squadron or something?"

"Aviation Squadron in Mascouche."

"Can you fly?"

"Yeah. I can fly."

"Like, for real?"

"With an instructor. Like getting a driver's license. I have to pass a test flight."

"Impressive. When does that happen?"

"Not sure yet," I say, feeling a tightness in my chest, partly from the heat and partly from picturing myself in a plane again.

"I'd never be brave enough to fly a plane," Dawn says.

"It doesn't take courage, really, just a lot of studying. Bravery is standing up to someone like Aimee without worrying about what she thinks."

"I worry plenty about what she thinks, maybe too much, but you can give as much as you get," Dawn says. "You got her to listen to you. I would have left her in the river."

"I don't believe that."

We get to a crossroads on the trail and I unfold the map again to be sure we head in the right direction. Aimee catches up to us, out of breath. Our attention is drawn upwards when we hear rumbling in the sky, again.

"Thunder?" Aimee asks.

I listen. "No. Too mechanical. It's a plane," I say.

"It's the plane from yesterday," Dawn points out.

She's right. Through the trees, we see it pass overhead and land somewhere upriver. I shiver, convinced the air is cooling around us. I have goose bumps on my arms.

"You all right?" Dawn asks, noticing.

"Yeah. Fine," I say. I keep the image of me in a cockpit trying to land with a crosswind, to myself. Instead, I take the trail that leads to the bridge and camp.

"I don't feel so great," Aimee says, sitting on a rock.

CHAPTER NINETEEN

Dizzy

"Guys, I need to rest," Aimee says. Her skin is grey. She's not as sweaty as before, which could be a sign she's dehydrated.

"Water?" I ask her.

"No. It's fine. Just give me a minute to catch my breath." Aimee holds her head in her hands. She looks terrible, and I don't want to push her to continue—especially since she can't monitor her blood sugar.

"Then eat something." I pull the wet peanut-butter sandwich out of my bag and offer it to Aimee, but she pushes my hand away.

"I don't feel like eating. I just need a rest."

"Oh, for god's sake. Drink some water and stop being so difficult," Dawn says, offering her water bottle.

Aimee accepts and takes a sip, but in no time, she's retching. The little water she drank comes back up, along with the protein bar.

"Shit. That can't be good," Dawn says.

"Aimee, listen to me," I say, once she's caught her breath. She has goose bumps, too, and is shivering. "You've stopped sweating. You're throwing up. You need to keep trying to drink. Small sips. Even if you throw up, again, or you'll get completely dehydrated."

"I can't," she says, desperate.

"A few breaths, then a little sip. It'll be fine," Dawn tells her. She doesn't look convinced, but offers the bottle again.

Aimee takes a small sip, and keeps it down for a minute before she's heaving again.

"We need help," I say.

"How?" Dawn asks.

"I can run to the medical cabin. It's not too far along the trail. There might be someone there, or a phone to call Jean-Paul. Will you stay with her?"

"Yeah, of course," Dawn says. "But, if she rests, and then can walk a little farther, we'll get to where the trails intersect before the med cabin. We're bound to find another group who can radio Jean-Paul. Then they can take care of her."

"The other teams might be way ahead of us. There's no guarantee we'll meet them. I don't want to risk it. I think the cabin is our best bet," I say.

"Okay, you're the cadet. We'll wait."

"Keep trying to get her to drink." Dawn gives me a thumb's up as I run down the trail, rolling thunder catching up to me.

CHAPTER TWENTY

Four Souls on Board

I'm pounding down the trail, remembering how we were taught in cadets to breathe while running. We went on plenty of runs, and if you want to conserve strength and oxygen, you need to focus on breathing. I slow down when a cabin with a red cross painted on the side comes into view. It's near the shore, where the amphibious plane we saw earlier bobs on its floaters.

"Hello?" I call, out of breath.

There's reggae music playing on a small radio. The cabin is no bigger than an outhouse, but when I look inside, I see it's shelved with first-aid equipment. Nearby, a man in a uniform lounges, sipping from a canteen. His shirt is white with a red cross on it.

"Thank god," I say. "I need help. Please."

He stands and approaches. "You alone?"

"No. I have two friends with me. Down the trail." I point. "One is diabetic. I think she's dehydrated. We need . . ." I bend over, my elbows on my knees, starting to feel faint myself.

". . . help."

"What's your name?" he asks, holding my elbow, supporting me.

"Marisa. I'm here with my school. We lost our communicator."

"I'm Thomas. All right; take it easy. Here." He offers me his canteen and I drink slowly. "Breathe. Show me." He grabs a first-aid kit and a folded stretcher.

*

I lead him to the spot where I left Dawn and Aimee. Aimee is lying on her side with Dawn crouched next to her, talking to her.

"Is she conscious?" Thomas asks.

"Yeah. Really weak, though," Dawn says, and for the first time I can hear the worry in her voice. Thomas crouches next to Aimee and asks her a few questions.

"I seriously thought she was going to pass out," Dawn says.

"She's gonna be okay," I say, finally feeling the tension in my entire body melt as Thomas speaks into his communicator. I recognize Jean-Paul's voice through the static on the other end.

Next, I hear Thomas communicate with someone else and I listen carefully. "Joliette this is Thomas at Camp Nord. I have a patient for transport who will need medical attention upon arrival."

"You're flying her?" I ask, looking at the overcast sky. The wind is picking up. It's cooled off quite a bit, which is a relief.

"We'll fly to the airport. An ambulance will take her to the hospital. Your teacher said he'll communicate with her parents and he'll meet us there and wait until her parents arrive."

"We don't all have to go," I say.

"Our credits," Dawn says.

"We can head back to camp on foot, can't we?" I ask Thomas. I know Aimee will be all right, and Dawn and I still have a hike to finish.

"No," Aimee says, rolling over. She's so pale and her eyes look darker, the skin around them sunken and purplish. "I don't want to go alone."

It's as if I've swallowed a wad of steel wool.

"Please come," Aimee asks.

I can't believe I'm going to forfeit this weekend. I can't believe we'll end up in summer school because Aimee had to get her feet wet. But when I look at her again, I know I can't leave her alone. She's scared. And sick—and for the first time ever, asking for my help. And she's doesn't seem ashamed to do it.

"Of course, I say."

"What about me?" Dawn asks, her arms at her sides, looking defeated.

"I can't leave you alone," Thomas says to Dawn.

"He's right," I say. "We'll both go."

Thomas unfolds the stretcher. With his instructions, it's easy to get Aimee to roll onto it, and the three of us carry her over the trails back to the cabin. We maneuver the stretcher onto the dock. With Thomas's support, Aimee is able to crawl into the backseat of the plane.

The wind has picked up. The temperature has dropped. I'm not sure if I'm shaking from cold or nerves. I remember the tarmac, the scrape of metal, the seatbelt digging into me, and Commander Hensen bleeding and unconscious.

"You can take shotgun," Dawn says, and sits next to Aimee.

I open the door and sit in the co-pilot seat. Fasten my seatbelt. I pull it to make sure it's secure. My pocket knife digs into my hip. Thomas checks fuel, flaps, emergency safety systems, and temperature. The outside temp has decreased to twenty-four degrees Celsius. It must have been much hotter when Aimee was in the river. Thomas configures his GPS. I notice the low-lying clouds in the distance. The mountains ahead. If this wasn't urgent, he might not take-off with the risk of storm clouds, but they are high enough to keep clearance above the mountains. It shouldn't take us more than fifteen minutes to get to the airport, but I know these are not ideal conditions. I check my seatbelt again as the engine starts and Thomas turns the plane upriver to prepare for take-off.

CHAPTER TWENTY-ONE

Turbulence

Thomas drives up one bank of the river and makes a U-turn to have enough room for take-off. Both banks of the river are rocky. If he doesn't maneuver slowly where the water is shallow, he won't see any rocks until we hit them. The wind has picked up and when we turn, it's on our tail, helping us move through the water and up into a smooth take-off.

The mountains poke through the clouds, and I worry there won't be enough clearance to get the right altitude without flying through cloud.

Aimee is still conscious, and Dawn is coaching her on sipping small amounts of water, which she's finally able to keep down without any dry heaving. She doesn't look great, and she's not talking, which is not like her. A ticking clock in my head reminds me she's been without insulin for over an hour.

At 1,000 feet, my ears pop. The cloud base has dropped and is already thick. Thomas can't go any higher or he'll lose visibility and maybe hit turbulence, and Aimee doesn't need to be bumped around in her condition. But with the mountains up ahead, the pilot will have to keep a safe altitude. The hills are lush and green, and although I'd love for us to have more distance between us and them, flying at half our maximum altitude is the safest bet for now. I watch the gauges as Thomas adjusts our altitude, as I would.

In the distance, more mountains jut upwards. Above the tallest hills, the clouds thicken; we won't have enough clearance. We can increase altitude, but the clouds descend into our flight path. We're already too close to the ground, and there is definitely going to be turbulence, but Thomas stays the course and keeps as low as he can; his eyes on the horizon. I don't know him, but he looks calm, and being next to someone so in control helps me remember to breathe. *Relax*. He's keeping us steady.

"Just a heads-up, ladies—we may hit a little turbulence, but the good news is . . ." He shifts to glance at his GPS.

"It won't last long," I cut in.

"Exactly. Brace yourselves for a little shifting. Puke bags are in the sleeve of the seat in front of you," he says over his shoulder to Dawn. "Yours is . . ." he pauses and points to the door.

"Right here," I say, opening the compartment in the door. "I'll be okay," I say.

As we reach the cloud base above the mountains, the plane vibrates. I grasp the armrest and hold tight as we're jostled around the plane. In a small aircraft like this one, any movement feels intense and amplified.

Thomas controls the plane's roll and pitch by holding the control column with one hand. With the other hand, he adjusts the throttle to recover from the bouncing. But seconds later, we're pitched nose up, the wings rolling up and down. In the next second, the plane drops. It's like riding a roller coaster in the fog—without the fun. I look at the monitor: we've dropped three-hundred feet. The force lifts us off our seats and back down with a bump. I don't get travel sickness, but this drop has me feeling queasy. Dawn lets out a yelp, and Aimee groans.

"Everyone all right back there?" Thomas asks.

"Uh-huh," Dawn says, opening a puke bag and holding it in front of Aimee. "Just in case," she says to me, but Aimee has enough energy to push it away.

"I'm fine," Aimee says, but her pale face and sunken eyes say otherwise.

"Just hang on," I say. "We're almost there." There's more turbulence and I hold onto my seatbelt, trying to keep from bumping into Thomas. He's a tall man, built, and our shoulders are touching, but I don't want to interfere with his maneuvering. When we start flying more smoothly, I let go, my fingers aching from hanging on so tightly.

Thomas regains our altitude and controls our pitch. The horizon is where it should be, but the engine is running roughly.

"What's that?" Dawn says, noticing the sensation. "It feels like we're stalling." Her hand is on my shoulder.

"What?" Aimee sits up, but she's not looking any better. Her face drains, and she leans back into her chair.

I place my hand on Dawn's, trying to be reassuring. She's trembling. "What's happening?" Dawn asks.

I stretch my neck out to look at the dash. Thomas notices my curiosity, but remains focused. "The temperature outside has dropped with the altitude we've gained. That, along with the intense humidity, means there might be icing on the carburetor."

"That's the engine?" Dawn asks.

"It mixes air and fuel for the engine," I correct her.

"So what happens if it gets iced?" Aimee asks. She looks weak and pale, but alert enough to follow the conversation.

There's a shudder throughout the plane, and then a lack of feeling.

The engine is stalling.

I turn back to Thomas. He checks the fuel mixture. There needs to be the right ratio of fuel to air in the carburetor. He makes sure the carburetor heat is on. Selects a different fuel valve. The ignitions are fine, left and right.

It's hard to describe an absence of sound. It's not silent, but there isn't the constant buzz and whirring there should be.

"What just happened?" Dawn asks.

"The engine stopped," I say.

"What the—" Dawn starts, but Thomas cuts her off.

"Just relax. This is going to be fine." He's so calm and collected, even though our engine has stopped mid-flight. "Marisa, how do you know that?" he asks me.

"Cadets."

"Great. What's next," he asks me, like this is a ground simulation, and we're not thousands of feet in the air in a stalled plane.

I remember my training. *Aviate. Navigate. Communicate.*

Aviate: I know what the problem is—icing. I know how to solve it, but it didn't work. "Start the engine. Check the mixture," I say.

Thomas verifies as I speak. "Mixture rich," he says.

"Throttle full open," I say. "Three pumps of primer to get fuel to the cylinders to start the engine. Turn ignition." He does each step in tandem as I call it. I think to breathe.

Still nothing.

"It won't start," I say.

Thomas nods, but he's calm. The girls in the back are stunned, watching and listening. Dawn has her hand over her mouth. Aimee has tears running down her face.

We're gliding, completely vulnerable to the winds around us.

Navigate: We're in the mountains. Beyond them there are fields where Thomas can land. There is a highway. We are north of the airport.

Communicate.

Thomas activates the radio.

"Mayday Mayday Mayday
This is Cessna one-eight-five
FOXTROT ROMEO ROMEO KILO
FOXTROT ROMEO ROMEO KILO
FOXTROT ROMEO ROMEO KILO
Engine failure. Emergency landing.
Five miles north of Joliette.
One-thousand feet. One-hundred-twenty KNOTS.
Four souls on board. FOXTROT ROMEO ROMEO KILO."

Thomas's voice is stern, quick, and clear.

I count to three and hope someone will respond.

There is static.

Then a voice.

"Mayday.
FOXTROT ROMEO ROMEO KILO
FOXTROT ROMEO ROMEO KILO
FOXTROT ROMEO ROMEO KILO.
This is Joliette tower.
Joliette tower.
Joliette tower.
Received Mayday."

They know where we are. They know where we're going. They know our trouble. But we have to land this plane.

CHAPTER TWENTY-TWO

Gliding

A plane can glide a few miles without the engine, but we won't make it to the airport.

"Fields," I say. "Two miles."

"Yup," Thomas answers.

The mountains lower into rolling hills then flatten into fields of green. The cloud base has risen, and we can see more clearly. The wind has died down and the turbulence has stopped. We've lost altitude, but we'll make it to the fields. It won't be graceful or smooth, but Thomas is a pro.

"What now?" Aimee asks. "The engine actually stopped?"

"I think we're sailing," Dawn says.

"Gliding," I correct her.

"You mean falling," Dawn says.

"Oh my god," Aimee yells. Her colour is still a grey-green, but her eyes are lit with terror.

"It's okay," Thomas says.

"We're prepared for this," I say. But I'm not the one flying. "Thomas is prepared for this."

Thomas pulls a lever, and we feel the vibration of the landing gear being deployed.

"What do we do?" Dawn asks.

"Stay calm. A plane won't just drop out of the sky. It is kind of like sailing. We use the winds to glide back down. But it'll be a rough landing. So, check your belts and brace yourselves for landing. Like this." I tuck my head in my lap with my feet flat on the floor and my hands behind my head. Aimee and Dawn do as I show them, but I sit back up.

Rock's words ring out at me: *You've got this.* Commander Hensen told me the same thing before my test flight. I fight the urge to take the controls to lower the flaps. Thomas does it half a second after I think it. He turns off the battery and fuel. I look straight ahead as we approach the fields and Thomas keeps us steady.

The sky is brighter, more white than grey, and there is less haziness on the horizon. The nose dips and rises. Thomas steadies the plane and my heart and stomach follow each dip. I keep my eyes open, although I want to shut them tight. From the back seat, I hear Aimee breathing heavily. When I turn my head to look at her, she and Dawn are crouched, like I showed them, a hand behind their head and their free hand locked into each other's.

The patches of green and gold fields rush up to meet us. The landing gear burrows into the soft earth. Aimee grunts softly on impact. We're on the ground. But I know we're not in the clear—not until the plane stops. Plants splay out, torn from the roots as we rip through some poor farmer's corn seedlings.

We come to an abrupt stop. Thomas's hands are still on the yoke. He looks at me and asks, "You okay?"

"Fine," I say.

"How about you two?" he asks Dawn and Aimee.

Aimee's head is still down. Dawn raises her head and looks out the window.

"We're safe?" Dawn asks.

"We are. Everything is fine," I say. "Told you," I tease.

A man comes running from the barn into the field toward us and I open the door. "Oh my god. Are you all right?"

Thomas opens his door and checks on Aimee in the back seat, while the man helps me out of the plane. A siren in the distance grows louder each moment until two ambulances arrive near the barn. Two first responders help maneuver Aimee out of the back seat and carry her away.

"You all right?" The paramedic asks Dawn, as she crawls out of her seat. I give her my hand to help. She looks stunned, her eyes focused on her feet, and she doesn't answer. She may be in shock.

Another paramedic comes to see us. "You two all right?" she asks.

"That was insane!" Dawn finally says. "But yeah, I'm okay. I'm fine. Where's Aimee?"

"They're taking your friend to the hospital. You two can drive with me," she says.

My feet are on solid ground. The plane is in one piece. We made it, but I still feel like I'm flying, for how light I feel. I haven't felt like this in a long time. But I come back down when I remember Aimee being rushed to the hospital.

CHAPTER TWENTY-THREE

Trust is a Three-Legged Race

The hospital is quiet, like in a horror movie just before the zombies jump out at the main character. A nurse comes in to check on Aimee, who is still sleeping. There are a few other people down the hall, but it's not like a hospital teeming with doctors running around saying *STAT*, like on TV. The nurse reads Aimee's vitals then leaves me sitting on the most uncomfortable chair in the world. Aimee is eerily quiet, too, until she starts to groan and flutter her eyelids. I'm on my feet next to her when she opens her eyes.

"Hey," I say.

She blinks a few times like she's trying to focus. Her eyes search the room then find me. Her hand goes to her head, but she becomes aware of the IV in her arm and moves the tube gently out of the way.

"What?" she croaks, her voice shaky and weak.

"You had us worried you were in a coma or something. They gave you insulin. You'll live." I try to sound funny, but she's still groggy. "They wanted to know who to call, but I didn't have any of your information, so Mr. Belisle is on the way. I think he called your parents."

"They won't come."

I step back in surprise. "What? Why?" I remember Aimee's mom when we were little. She always had cookies in the cupboard and let us watch movies on sunny days. I don't remember much about her dad, but I think her parents split up a while ago. I don't know what her history is with her parents, but something is strained.

She swallows hard and it looks painful. I pour her a cup of water.

"It's a long story, but I've been staying with Natasha for the last few weeks. They should call her mom to get me."

"Your parents should know what happened," I say. Aimee shifts in the bed, trying to get comfortable. "If they know what happened, I'm sure they'll come," I say, although I have no way of knowing if that's true.

"Maybe. But I rather they didn't."

As meddlesome and annoying as my mom is, I can't imagine not wanting her here if I were hurt. "Okay. I'm sorry."

"I mean, it's temporary, but we needed a break from each other. I needed some space; they are way too controlling."

"How's it been working out at Natasha's?" I ask.

"Turns out her mom is just as strict as mine. But not as good a cook." She half smiles at me. She stares at the generic painting behind me: a pot of purple flowers. Lilacs, I think.

"They said they'll get you hooked up with a new insulin pump," I say, changing the subject.

"Yeah. But I can't believe I lost my bag. My life was in that bag."

"It can all be replaced," I tell her.

"I guess."

I realize Aimee's overstuffed bag is what she's been living out of. I feel bad for her, but her face is still cold and tough, and I don't know what to say.

"I can't believe we flew in that little plane," she says.

"You've never flown?" She shakes her head. "Then I should take you up sometime, when you're better."

Her eyes go wide. "You fly?"

I nod, but I don't explain how I don't technically have my license, yet. There's a long pause where we listen to the nurses chatting outside the room.

Aimee sips from her glass, then says, "So, you like a superhero or something?" Her words don't have the usual bitterness and sarcasm attached. Her hair is down around her face. Her eyes are sleepy, with dark circles underneath. Her skin is oily and she looks a little grey, but she's smiling. Her voice is soft and genuine. This is where she hides her beauty.

"Not at all," I say. "I ran for help. Who wouldn't?"

"Anyone who knows me." The beauty melts into sadness. "Thanks," she says, before I can argue. "Think we'll get our credits even though we didn't finish the hike?"

"We survived, so I think we can bet on it."

*

Natasha and her mom show up a few hours later. I leave them talking with Aimee in her room and meet Dawn in the lobby, who is saying goodbye to Thomas.

"I just came to check in on everyone, but the nurse says your friend will be fine," Thomas says.

"Yeah, she's awake now. She'll be going home soon," I say. "Thanks, for everything."

"Yeah, that was crazy," Dawn says. "I still can't believe it."

"It's part of the job. Take care, you two." Thomas salutes, and walks off.

Dawn and I sit next to each other on a bench outside. "That was scary," she says.

I picture Thomas navigating the plane as though he read my mind each step of the way. I wasn't scared. I was . . . in control. "It was intense," I say.

"When the plane shut off, you knew exactly what was happening? You and Thomas were, like, synchronizing, or something."

"I know my stuff—in theory."

"And in practice?" she asks.

"Almost. It's a bit of a mess."

"Want to talk about it?" she asks.

Surprisingly, I do. I want to talk about it with her. I tell her the details only Rock, Mom, and the cadets know. She listens to my test-flight story without questions or interruptions. She must be curious, but she lets me talk, and saying it aloud actually feels good. When I get to the part about Commander Hensen being wheeled off in an ambulance, Dawn takes my hand. Her fingers are warm, but not clammy. They curl around my hand, and our fingers hook together. We sit on the bench, silent for a while, connected.

Mr. Belisle approaches us. He's sweaty, and looks worried.

"She's fine," I say. "Natasha's mom is already here. She'll take her home when they release her."

He doesn't say anything as we follow him to the parking lot. He points a set of car keys to the door of a pick-up truck with *Camp Du Nord* printed on the side.

At camp, everyone has about a million questions, but the only person who knows I'm not in the mood to answer them is Dawn, and she tells everyone to lay off in her not-so-gentle way. "Marisa figured a regular hike in the woods was too easy," she says.

I laugh. "You know me; always seeking adventure."

"Actually, I don't. Know you, I mean. Not much, anyway. But I'd like to." She reaches her hand to mine. I let her touch my hand and curl my fingers into hers, not caring if anyone notices. Our arms are swinging gently together when Jean-Paul approaches.

"Okay, everyone. Tonight's challenge is a nighttime three-legged race, so partner up with someone you trust and tie your legs together.

Without a word, Dawn grabs the rope from Jean-Paul and ties it around our legs in a sheet knot.

"Where'd you learn that?" I ask.

"Scouts, remember?" she answers with a grin.

CHAPTER TWENTY-FOUR

Home

The next morning, we get our cell phones back. I dial Rock's number to video chat the second we're on the bus.

"So, did you make it?" he asks. "You're still alive? You didn't kill Aimee, did you?"

"Almost, but it wasn't my fault. I swear," I say.

Next to me, Dawn laughs. I point my phone so Rock can see her, too. Dawn rests her head on my shoulder and waves to Rock.

"Hey, Dawn," he says, and she buries her head in her book. Rock's mouth opens in an exaggerated *WOW*. Thankfully, he doesn't say anything else about me sitting with Dawn. The bus rolls on, and we bump with each pothole, making it hard to keep my phone still.

"Does this mean you graduate?" Rock asks. "We can reschedule a test flight?"

"We'll get our credits, so that's one less worry. Will you help me review for the test flight?" I ask him.

"Absolutely."

"I don't think you need to study too hard," Dawn says. "You know your stuff."

"What does that mean?" Rock asks, excited. "What did you do?"

"You're not going to believe what happened yesterday."

"Can't wait to hear it," he says.

As we roll down the highway away from gravel roads and away from camp, Dawn and I tell him the whole story. By the end of it, Rock is beaming like a proud parent. It feels good—like where I belong—sitting next to this cool, strange girl, and talking about flying like it's a part of me again.

I've found the courage to fly again. I remember how much I love it. It's a feeling I want to chase for the rest of my life—no matter how much turbulence there may be.

Acknowledgements

It is with immense gratitude that I thank the Canada Council of the Arts. It is with their support that I was able to take the time to create this novel.

There are so many people involved in creating one little book. First, thank you to Lori Shwydky and Cheryl Ann Kelly from Rebel Mountain Press, whose guidance and kindness allowed this story to take full form.

To the authors I admire who read my idea, my outline and my manuscript, who gave me solid feedback, and helped shape and reshape the story: Liana Cusmano, Darlene Madott, Raquel Rivera, Amber Smith, Lori Weber, and Tim Wynne-Jones. I am most fortunate for their collaboration.

Monique Polak, thank you for making me feel like I can do anything, for all your fabulous advice, and for always returning my phone calls!

Maureen Marovitch, thank you for always answering my emails, and for writing with me during those lonely pandemic lockdowns.

To Allister Thompson for reading my manuscript and seeing its potential, and then, so kindly offering ways to make it stronger.

Victoria Berry, former student, for accepting to help me put together some facts and details about Aimee's character.

To Keith Saulnier, pilot, writer and kind stranger who answered my aviation questions.

To Linda Reilly, pilot, for editing the aviation sections with her expert eye.

To my student, Jack Carroll, for reading and rereading my blurb, when you should have been doing your English work.

To my husband, Sébastien, and our children Patrick, Dylan and Éloïse, thank you for not always respecting the "Do Not Disturb" rule as I wrote.

To my parents and siblings, who always cheer me on. Your support is everything.

Finally, and with most pride, to Thomas Simo, my nephew. Thank you for reading my words, correcting mistakes about aviation and answering every one of my texts. Most of all, thank you for taking me flying. It was the only time I've enjoyed the experience, and it is thanks to you and your passion that this novel took its first breath.

Thank you.

*The author gratefully acknowledges the support of the
Canada Council for the Arts*

Canada Council　　　Conseil des arts
for the Arts　　　　 du Canada

About the Author

Lea Beddia is an author, storyteller and educator. Born and raised in Montreal, she now teaches in Joliette, Quebec, where she lives with her husband and three children. When she isn't writing for teenagers, she's likely watching zombies take over the world, eavesdropping on conversations, or baking something with too much chocolate. She wanted to be a superhero when she was younger, but will settle for creating characters who can change the world. Her missions are to create accessible literature for striving readers, and to find the best gelato on the planet. She will not give up on her quest for either.

Visit her at www.leabeddia.com
and Facebook or Instagram @BeddiaLea